Cloudy Trophies

ANNE GOODWIN WINSLOW

ALFRED A. KNOPF · NEW YORK · 1946

FIRST EDITION

TO THE MEMORY OF RICHARD STEELE

Ay, in the very temple of delight
Veil'd Melancholy has her sovran shrine,
Though seen of none save him whose strenuous tongue
Can burst Joy's grape against his palate fine;
His soul shall taste the sadness of her might
And be among her cloudy trophies hung.

KEATS: ODE ON MELANCHOLY

CLOUDY TROPHIES

I The Pond

SOME YEARS AGO, when Washington was a smaller place, a lady living in one of the quiet houses around Lafayette Square could on a summer evening throw a bit of lace over her head and, gathering up her skirts, step across the street into that shady precinct almost as casually as she would go into her garden. She might not even raise her eyes in doing it, so negligible in those days were either the dangers or the distractions of the thoroughfare.

Mrs. Richard Steele was rather in the habit of doing this. Lafayette Square in the spring was almost like the country, she said; she had been raised in the country; and as the summer advanced, if Congress was late in adjourning, she found that sitting on one of the ornamental iron seats under the trees and well back from the gravel walk was a good deal like sitting on the lawn at home. The trees were the same kind as the ones that grew down there. She and Senator Steele were both from the South.

From under the low branches of the elm where her favorite seat was located she could see the clipped green space in the center of the Square where General Jackson rode his rocking-horse, but not the General. The nursery statue—her husband called it that—was neatly hidden behind a clump of laurels; which made it easier to imagine the round open place might be the pond at home, where the lawn sloped down to the fence and the wood-lot beyond.

Not very many people walked through Lafayette Square in those days though it was always the nicest way to cut across from Pennsylvania Avenue; at least not too many. Passing footsteps did not often break the thread of Mrs. Steele's reflections, nor did passing attention. She was not apt to be overlooked wherever she was and would not have expected it to happen here. There may be even today a few people who remember the lady in a summer dress sitting, with a book she was not reading, clear against the dark trees.

"Laura never reads books," her husband said. "That's what makes me love her. It would be dreadful if she did."

4

"What would it do to her?" Sabrina Halliday, who was Laura's cousin, inquired.

"Just what it does to everybody; just what you'd expect. Everybody reads books, everybody must be given—that means sold—books that he will read. The common denominator, Sabrina, should be thwarted wherever possible. Laura is thwarting it."

The front windows of the house on H Street overlooked the Square, and the long parlor where Senator and Mrs. Steele entertained their guests was full of pleasant lights and shadows. It was not in the least what would be called today the living-room. Laura preferred to live upstairs, where she could have window-boxes and her canary bird. There she enjoyed changing things about and admiring the changes; the parlor had to be just so. Sabrina Halliday had gradually taken over the downstairs part of the housekeeping, now that she had, gradually too, come to live with them. Sabrina was young, but she had been keeping house for somebody ever since she was born, she said. She knew just how the tall windows and the crystal chandeliers had to be "done" to keep them shining, as well as all those lower objects they shone upon, which

5

were many in those days and called for many different kinds of doing. "Ferns in the fern-dish, fires in the fireplace—what a brain!" Senator Steele liked to joke about it, but he also liked knowing that he had one of the "charming homes" in Washington.

A home where the cook was taught to cook and dinner guests were almost a daily occurrence, though dinner parties remained as far apart as he could keep them. "Must we have a party, Laura?"

"But only two more people, Richard; does that make it a party? It's no more trouble, is it, Sabrina?"

"He knows it's not. He doesn't go by that. What do you go by, anyhow?"

"The weather-glass, Sabrina. Atmospheric disturbances are bound to follow what you are planning to do. There'd be lightning in the hall as soon as we let them in, and thunder in the coat closet; old Royce's sombrero would start jumping on the First Secretary's top hat. At least you can wait until this South American business settles down a little."

Coming downstairs in the morning before the servants had restored their daytime aspect to the rooms, Sabrina always wondered at the abandoned look they wore, so disproportionate to any revels they had wit·

6

nessed. If the guests had spilled their wine and flung
their wreaths about, the morning light when she let
it in could not seem more of an intrusion. Something
withdrew before it; something that would go off and
hide. Were there ghosts at every social gathering?
Couldn't even these few friends meet together, and
talk and laugh and like each other, without letting
something in to stand behind their chairs—something
that would not stay?

Whose lights are fled,
Whose garlands dead—

She sang softly to herself, folding back the inside
blinds and picking up Laura's little handkerchief
from the rug. The satin pillow in the corner of the
sofa where Nora Digby had sat still wore the print of
her shoulder. Mrs. First Secretary. Anybody could
recognize the dents Nora left, even if they didn't whiff
her perfume, she thought, shaking the pillow up and
sniffing the ghost of Nora. Not of itself but thee. A
man in love with a woman like Nora would have a
lot to agonize over if he ever lost her. Sabrina
imagined the Honorable Cecil: Menelaus weeping
over Helen's dents in the mattress. What sensualists

the classic poets were! Or was it just her father, who always dwelt on passages like that when he was teaching her? Or maybe she was the one, for always remembering them. *Veteris vestigia flammæ*—but that was Venus, not Helen. Anyhow, Nora left plenty of *vestigia.*

Sabrina turned, and a mirror in a deep gold frame that reached from floor to ceiling between the two windows caught up the room with her in it and held them in a meaning of its own. There she was, in her blue dress, with her red hair—yes, and her brain—in some sort of relation to all those other objects: able to move them around, to do things with them, but not things that affected them really; not to soak them with her personality, the way Nora Digby did, or Laura, or the Senator for that matter. She didn't touch them with romance as the others did. Sabrina wished sometimes she were not so practical.

The house she had kept for her father was rented now. It was after he died that she had begun staying with Laura. At that time she and the Senator, not a Senator yet, were living on their plantation. Then she had begun coming to Washington with them, and now when she spoke of going home it was their home she meant—back to the plantation. They always managed to spend part of the summer there, so the Senator could look after his crops and his constituents. And "after" was exactly what he meant, he said, because the only look he ever got was after they had both gone to the devil.

It was hot at the plantation, naturally, but then it was hot in Washington too by that time, and at least the country looked cooler, Laura said, and she had always lived there. Laura seemed to think of that part of her life—the pre-urban part—as if it stretched back indefinitely into the past. Sabrina wondered how many years of cosmopolitan existence—if Washington was that—it would take to get Laura even into the present tense. She practically never mentioned the future, or looked forward to anything beyond the summer. Laura ought to go to things more than she did; if she didn't like calls and receptions, there were always the concerts and the art exhibitions. If only the Senator had more time—"Why don't you call Richard 'Richard,' Sabrina?"

Laura had about stopped asking her that. He still reminded her now and then that in addressing him *Mr.* Senator was the correct form, but for one thing

he was so much older than she was. She could remember thinking he was too old for Laura to marry,
which was absurd of course: he was only forty-seven
now. Laura had really changed more than he had;
but that was on account of Rickie; she took it so much
harder.

The lawn at the side of the house sloped down to
the fence, and beyond that was the wood-lot with the
pond almost in the middle of it. It was not deep, but
it had always seemed to Laura that having the trees
reflected in it from top to bottom that way made it
just any depth you chose to imagine. All the water
down at the plantation was dark, though it was sometimes quite clear, like coffee. It was the cypress trees
that made it that way, everybody said, but the trees
around the pond were mostly sweet gums. Not even
maples take on such crimson as they do in the fall, and
for some reason the leaves look redder reflected in the
water than they do on the trees.

A little farther on, where the ground sloped up
again, was the house where the cook lived—generally
Mattie. Mattie loved to piece quilts; she had been doing it for years, out of all the scraps she could lay her

hands on. Her quilts were a regular family tree of all the dresses everybody had ever had, and when Laura walked over there with Rickie and saw them hanging out on the fence around her little log house—to "catch the air" Mattie called it—they could both recognize their own scraps. Rickie's were nearly always the blue ones; she never could understand how his eyes and hair could be like that, so blue and gold, when she and his father were neither of them blond. It made it seem somehow as if he didn't really belong to them; as if they didn't have the right to just claim him that way—

"It's his great-grandmother claiming him," Richard said; "the one hanging over the sofa in the parlor. She's maintaining her famous complexion by the long arm of the Mendelian law. They say she used to wear veils and things all summer long. Imagine it, Laura, in this heat! Wait till his little sister comes along. She'll probably be such a nut-brown baby you won't want to claim her either." But the little sister had never come. She was beginning to think God did not want to give them children, as He did to almost everybody else. Only to lend them that one, for those few years.

Mattie's quilts were not much to look at when you saw them close, but from a little distance, hanging out in the woods that way, and especially in the autumn, when they seemed to match the trees, they looked simply gorgeous; you could hardly believe your eyes. It was like something in a Wagner opera; Kundry's garden; or in a fairy-tale. "Look what a beautiful magic Mattie has made!" she and Rickie used to say when they saw them. They pretended Mattie was a witch and hung them out that way to draw people into the woods; but only a good witch of course: the kind that made cakes for little boys. Mattie went home every afternoon to "take her ease" as she called it, before she came to get dinner, and Rickie loved to visit her. But he was never allowed to go by himself, on account of the pond.

Laura had stopped trying to think how he ever happened to go there by himself that afternoon. She had had to stop, because she was getting so she couldn't think of anything else; all day, and especially all night, her mind went over and over it. It had been such a little while since she had seen him riding his new velocipede round and round the lawn, right where she could watch him from the window. It was easy

to see him in his little red cap and sweater that he insisted on wearing, hot as it was, because they were
new too; she had just bought them for him the day
before. She was sewing upstairs in her room and
called to him out the window that she would be down
directly and they would go for a walk. That must
have made him think of going to Mattie's house, and
then, for some reason that she had never been able to
work out, he must have just suddenly decided to go
by himself. He had ridden his velocipede a little way
down the slope toward the fence and left it there; but
he had not gone to Mattie's; she had been there all the
time, she said, and had not seen him. And nobody had
heard him, still as the whole place was at that time of
day. Jake was supposed to be working in the garden,
but he might have been asleep; it was very warm for
October. Jake was the one who told her. Everybody
was looking by that time; when she missed him and
he didn't answer, she thought of course he must be in
the garden with Jake, and then Jake had run over to
ask Mattie. When he saw his little red cap on the
water, Jake said at first he thought it was a sweet gum
leaf.

But although she had stopped thinking about it as

much as she used to, she still felt that the thing she couldn't bear was not to know how it happened. Not why; she had sense enough not to ask that. God didn't tell people why; but they ought to be able to figure out for themselves just what mistake they or somebody else had made. It was an afternoon just like all the others, with everybody doing the things he always did, and then something, maybe some very little thing, must have happened to change it. If she could only know what—

"But think of all the other things you would have to know in order to know that," her husband said. "The mystery of coincidence is one of the greatest of them all, Laura."

Surely, he thought, she must learn in time that grief, like every other human thing, cannot be left to go its own way, or where should we be led? But it would be three years now, in October.

And this was May. The parks in Washington were full of tulips, and so were Laura's window-boxes; yellow ones to match the curtains; and Coq d'Or swinging in the cage above them, added his little yellow note to all his other coruscations.

14

"Does he never run down and have to be wound up?" Nora Digby inquired, rather in the spirit of criticism, for she was talking. Nora had had a very interesting life, and what good would it be to her, Sabrina said, if she couldn't talk about it? Most of it had been spent in India. "Which may be the reason I feel about the English as I do," she said. "They are much worse out there. Insufferable, really."

Nora apparently considered this statement a tribute to the Englishman who, in spite of being one and being out there, had succeeded in marrying her. She had been born in India, but both her parents were from County Clare.

"And what becomes of the little mango tree?" Laura asked her. Laura was always interested in Nora's interesting life. "Does the fakir just go off and leave it there?"

"He will if you want to have it," Nora said. "Some people think it is unlucky; but in any case it hardly ever lives very long."

"But you can't believe it, Nora—that a tree could just grow up all of a sudden like that! You know it must be hypnotism—or something."

"Something, by all means," Nora said. "It's always so easy to believe in something. For my part, I prefer to believe my eyes."

Laura looked at Nora's eyes. They were gray with very dark lashes; her loveliest feature; but they did not look as if they would see things unless the things were there. Nora was intelligent; even Sabrina admitted that she was intelligent; and yet the things she managed to believe!

"Don't listen to her, Mrs. Steele. She is trying to make you as crazy as she is." The Honorable Cecil was always joking about it, and so was Richard, but Nora just kept right on telling things as if everybody believed them as much as she did—or would, by the time she had told them enough.

She did not keep on about the mango tree, however; she had only brought it up because she had seen one that morning in the Botanical Garden, on her way back from the Capitol. Nobody could say Nora ought to go to more things than she did: even the Botanical Garden, even Congress, whose open sessions were in those days more openly arrived at. She didn't have to have a ticket; she just drifted in and sat down where she pleased, and that was, whenever possible, in what she was pleased to call her seat, in the front row of the Senate gallery.

"The Senator was in top form this morning," she told Laura. "Amusing, really."

"I know," Laura said; "he always makes people laugh. But the other side doesn't like it. I believe they hate it worse than anything. I wish Richard cared more than he does about making enemies."

"But that is very stupid of you, Laura. What would you expect him to make, right in the middle of a fight? He has his friends lined up already."

"I know," Laura said again, "but all the same—"

"And the openings his opponents give him! He simply has to take them. It is amazing," Nora went on, "the clumsy minds you send to Congress—or does one say *the* Congress? That Voltz fascinates me though. 'My God, can it be possible!' I say every time he opens his mouth. Talk about not believing your eyes; that is one case where you cannot believe your ears."

"It isn't only his voice," Laura said. "I wonder sometimes if he can be possible himself. And right now, with everybody getting so stirred up over that boundary dispute, and the President's message and all, he can do a lot of harm saying those things. Richard says he has a regular Jefferson Brick vocabulary. Richard thinks what the President said was bad enough."

" 'To resist by every means in our power any willful aggression on the part of England—' poor old dear!" Nora laughed. "I asked Cecil if I should begin right away to pack." She picked up her gloves and her parasol from the chair beside her. "All right, you noisy bird, I yield the floor," she said, throwing a kiss at the cage. "But I do hope you are going to the Wootens' dinner, Laura. Cecil may need your husband's help; the lion's tail, you know. I wonder who else will be there? It's rather awkward for the hostesses who got out invitations before all this came up."

Richard Steele was in the habit of explaining the fact that he knew German and admired Goethe with a thoroughness no American education ever imparted, by telling people he had spent his student years in Germany. If they were interested he might go on to tell them that the years had been only two, because that was all he could afford, and that he had spent them at the University of Aachen rather than at Harvard, where his father and his grandfather had gone, because it was cheaper and had a less alien atmosphere. His youth had coincided with the period in Southern history when reconstruction politics had succeeded in bringing about an estrangement which Grant's armies had been unable to effect.

By the same agency a superior devastation had been accomplished. The fields his ancestors had tamed and tended would have seemed to them, by the time they came into his hands, the glebe of strangers, but to the boy they had not ceased to wear the features of a friend. Hope could still be planted in that deep soil, and they were at least something he could borrow money on until he could do something else.

A degree in philosophy and literature from a German university was not the something else. For that, too, debt would have to be incurred; to himself this time; a certain number of years—those two—and an uncertain amount of energy expended. On all of which the return he vaguely contemplated was to result eventually from the practice of law in his native State.

"And so," he said, "I prepared myself to be a local

lawyer and politician by sitting on the tomb of Char-
lemagne reading Goethe."

Since, however, almost the only thing that can be
said with certainty about any preparation is that it
leads on to another one, until at the margin of his own
tomb a man may be able to say where they all have
led, it is possible Steele did not consider those two
years quite the deviation he liked to represent them.
As a stage or merely a step in any career he could
imagine for himself, their value even at the time was
not apparent, but to the one he actually followed they
gave a direction he could not afterward imagine it
without.

"People keep saying you are the only man in the
South whose opinions would be listened to in Washington. I wonder how they know what your opinions really are, Richard?" Laura's schooling in the
language of politics had begun and the long evenings
at the plantation were never long enough for her husband's friends to finish talking to him and go home.

"Maybe they just want me to know theirs," he said.

"But theirs seem to have so little weight with you
either. You treat everything so lightly, Richard."

"The law of gravitation doesn't always apply in

matters of judgment, Laura—outside of a German lecture-room at least. Intelligence works just as well in most cases; or even taste."

Laura smiled, not so much at the words as because he was smiling; treating her opinion lightly now.

Those were the days when she listened for hours to the voices that rose and fell outside on the porch, while she sat by the lamp in the parlor sewing on Rickie's little clothes. The only other sound in all the miles of summer darkness that fell away on every side was the noise of insects in the trees, and now and then a bull-frog in the pond; or somebody's horse tied to the fence, whinnying because he knew how late it was. The ruffled white curtains at the windows that reached from floor to ceiling moved in and out between her and the voices and the cigar smoke and the occasional sputter of a match. How could it be so interesting so long? To Richard too, in spite of all he said. But in the end it ended; the last horse was untied; the last voice rode away.

"How can they take you seriously, Richard, when you never are?" He was still smiling at something as he stepped through the long window out of the soft darkness into the soft light.

"Why should I be serious about the things that have nothing, or so little, to do with you?" He came behind her and leaned over until his face touched her hair. "When the only really serious thing in the world anyhow is just the one the *ewig* man says to the *ewige* woman in those three words?"

The two dark heads together in the lamplight were very much alike, in spite of Steele's graying forelock. They could both see the resemblance in the mirror opposite; they knew already it was there. "You two look too much like brother and sister to have ever got married." Sabrina said that sometimes even now.

Nora had noticed too that they looked alike. "The first time I ever saw you," she told Laura—"standing together near the door of the drawing-room at the Embassy—do you remember? It was the first one of Lady Mildred's ghastly receptions after we came, and I was 'assisting' her. Trust the English for the stodgiest parties known to man! And there I was, in line, with no hope of getting out of it, unless I could faint, or maybe die. 'Who are they?' I asked Lady Mildred when you came in. You had on that white chiffon I always liked better than any other dress I ever saw you wear, and your pearl necklace that was your mother's. I hope you will go on wearing white, Laura; you ought never to wear anything else—" She stopped. "Isn't it a funny thing," she began again, "that I can never think of you as anything but young? Even when I try to imagine you looking like a 'matron' you just refuse to be one."

Laura smiled. "Nobody in my family ever seems to get fat," she said.

"I don't mean just heavier—" Nora closed her eyes. "It's a question of vibrations," she said, opening them. "But I noticed then how much you looked like each other; it was one of the things that interested me. It means a great deal, Laura, when that happens. The soul, you know—or perhaps you have never thought much about those things—but every individual soul is like a traveler going on an endless journey, stopping at one resting-place, one incarnation we say, after another; choosing always the one that is most fitting— that it best deserves. So you see when two people have progressed by the same stages and arrive together at an equal point of development, how natural it is that they should resemble one another in every way. Naturally too they recognize each other as destined companions, or affinities, as people say. It would be impossible for it to be otherwise. Sabrina is foolish to talk about brother and sister, which is an accidental thing; this is the result of the most profound intention," Nora said.

Laura listened in silence. Nora's ideas were beautiful, and if her intention was sometimes too profound to follow without a little practice, that didn't keep it from being interesting.

" 'Many a house of life has held me,' " she quoted. "It was Buddha who said that; and naturally, so long as we are in the house we can only see one another through the windows; but as we advance, as we step outside, the windows will become unnecessary; we will not have to take them around with us in order to recognize each other, or even to see what is happening to someone far away. Some day we will no longer need our eyes at all. It has happened to me often already; I have told you about it; I will suddenly see a place that I was not thinking of at all, or a person, with great clearness. And then I can be always sure that something is happening or is about to happen that will be in some way connected with what I have seen—" She stopped suddenly and began to laugh.

"Did I tell you about the time I saw what was happening at my friend's house in Russia?"

Laura shook her head. "When, Nora? Since you have been here—in Washington?"

Nora nodded. "I was sitting in my room, fixing my hair and not thinking of Russia at all, and not of Irène—that is her name—when I began to see her house in the country, where I have often been, almost as if it were there in the mirror in front of me, and I knew that something was happening because her little girls were crying. And then I saw it was for their governess that the tears were: Mademoiselle Victoire, who had always been with them, quite an old maid, but good, and they were devoted to her. I could see her all in white with white flowers, and there were people all around. It made me very sad, I assure you, Laura, and I wrote to Irène to say how sorry I was that they had lost poor Mademoiselle; and can you imagine my surprise when she wrote back to say it was by a wedding and not a funeral that she had been lost! Even now I find it difficult to believe in Mademoiselle Victoire as a bride like that, arrayed as if she were the youngest virgin; and you should have heard the way Cecil made fun of me when I told him—"

Nora's esoteric wanderings were apt to terminate like this, in a field of reminiscence that might be thought more shadowy still. "For my part," Sabrina said, "I don't see much choice between what she considers her ideas and what she wants you to consider her experiences. They seem to me about equally fabulous. How many of those things she tells you do you believe, Laura?"

"I just think they're interesting," Laura said. "Maybe it's the way she tells them; and I do believe she believes them or she couldn't tell them that way."

"But the Senator is mistaken: I would not deprive him of his opinions simply because it amazes me that a man in this day and age should hold them, any more than I would deprive him of his life for the reason that he happens to be that man. It is his epoch I object to: it confuses evolution; it upsets Darwin. But I would not exterminate the Senator merely because I believe he should already have been extinct for ages." (Laughter.)

Laura put the paper down; she had read it twice already, and every time the doorbell rang or she heard voices in the hall she was sure it was Nora coming to tell it to her all over again. "The situation is getting pretty tense, Laura. Everybody knows Voltz isn't going to go on letting your husband maul him this way indefinitely. He may miss some of the fine points and a lot of the references, but he is nobody's fool." Nora said those things as if she had been to the theater or a Roman holiday or something. If it were her husband—

The picture Laura's imagination drew of Nora's well-appointed husband delivered over, Oxford accent and all, to the potentialities embodied in the Honorable Theodore F. Voltz somehow turned out to be diverting. She could smile at it because she knew it was the kind of thing that did not happen. Why did Richard always have to get people so stirred up about him one way or the other? They either worshiped the ground he walked on and did everything he wanted them to, or else they resented him and opposed him at every turn, and sometimes ended by actually hating him. He seemed to consider it a kind of game. Politics was a game, maybe, but Richard played with people's feelings. Imagine the way Senator Voltz must feel, reading this in the paper and remembering the way everybody had laughed!

And he must be thinking already of something he could do to get even with Richard. She didn't believe either one of them, or the people in the galleries either, thought half as much about what happened down in South America as they did about what was happening on the floor of the Senate, now that things had taken this personal turn. Richard and Senator Voltz used at least to pretend to be friends socially even if they were political enemies. As short a while back as the Wootens' dinner they were joking with each other about the border dispute and calling it "that Boston Tea Party down on the equator," but now nobody would dream of asking them to dinner together.

Laura could look back with satisfaction on that dinner, so ill-timed for General and Mrs. Wooten, to whom its possibilities of disaster were more apparent than they were to her. It was not the first time the General had seen reason to deplore his wife's partiality for what he called a mixed party. Any party in Washington was hazardous enough, in his opinion, even if you stuck to the two arms of the service and a few innocuous civilians, where at least you were familiar with the ground and had only the natural lines of cleavage to look out for; but this thing of trying to incorporate the diplomatic set, and especially the administration crowd—

The evening had started badly too. It had been one of those occasions where for some reason it was hard to assemble the parts. Instead of the steady roll of carriage wheels following one another in quick succession upon the stroke of half past seven, there had been intervals between the arrivals at the door, followed by suspended greetings in the drawing-room, and finally a cessation of such activities altogether, that was still not followed in its turn by the announcement of dinner. A lot of those people didn't even know the rules, General Wooten reflected, closing the hunting case of his watch carefully without snapping it; for Senator Voltz to be more than half an hour late was under the circumstances an outrage. All this political tension was bad enough without scrapping etiquette.

Mrs. Wooten, more concerned with domestic tensions, was rather in favor of scrapping the Senator; patience in these matters was not nearly so apt to be rewarded as the end of patience; she was in the act of murmuring to her husband under cover of an audible remark that she had told Jackson to announce dinner, when Senator Voltz was announced instead.

His excuses, whether or not they were acceptable to his host and hostess, were at all events not audible to the other guests, who were permitted to seek their respective places at the long table in an equal state of unenlightenment as to why they had not done it sooner. With perhaps a single exception; Nora, who went in with Steele, had made as she took his arm the singular statement that she knew what had happened and would tell him when she got a chance. "I believe it will surprise you," she said, stopping beside her own chair.

"I haven't a doubt of it," he said, pulling it out for her. "The things you tell me always do."

Nora let this pass while she got pushed in and arranged her skirts and unfolded her napkin and took a sip of water. "I believe it rather concerns you, too," she said then. " 'Something to your advantage;' at any rate you can turn it to your advantage."

"Would it be to my advantage to know how you heard it? You could tell me that right away, couldn't you—without getting a chance?" He was smiling at her, but she was serious.

"I didn't hear it at all," she said; "I saw it—as I was coming here."

"With your first sight or your second?"

"And how would I know that?"

"Did Cecil see it too? That would be one way, wouldn't it?"

"I didn't come with Cecil. He had to stop at the Embassy, so I came in one of those hired things—those victorias."

"So witness number one is out. Any others?"

"Rather. It happened right in the middle of Pennsylvania Avenue."

"In that case the papers will have it, won't they? When I read it in the morning will it still concern me?"

"Everything doesn't get put in the papers," Nora said.

"Not astral occurrences certainly. You mean—"

"Not at all. I mean it is always possible to keep things out of the papers, if one doesn't mind taking the time, or spending the money—or keeping the dinner waiting."

"Oh come now, Mrs. Digby!" Steele glanced around the table and then looked down again at Nora, but she had turned her attention to the gentleman on her left.

The events that Senator Voltz presumably did not want to figure in the newspapers seemed to Steele, when she recounted them, very unlikely to figure anywhere except in Nora's conversation. To have seen a woman in a black silk dress lying in the middle of the street and feebly waving a pair of white kid gloves— Come now, Mrs. Digby! But the gray eyes looked candidly back at him from the shadow of Nora's lashes.

"Quite plainly, really; it was not at all dark, you know—hardly seven o'clock yet—and at first there were very few people; no crowd, not even a policeman. It must have just that moment happened; they were just beginning to come."

"Not dead, I hope; don't make her dead, Mrs. Digby," Steele said.

"She was moving her hands; I told you that," Nora said. "My cabby had already stopped his horse; he was getting down to see if he could do anything, when a man began pointing to a carriage that was just turning out of the avenue into that street there by the Treasury, and calling out: 'Yonder goes the guy that did it!' and then—"

Admiration at this point began to get the upper

hand in her listener's attention, and Nora was allowed to proceed for a minute or two without protest. He listened while the policeman gave the signal and the carriage, a closed one, "very *comme il faut*," was turned back and its occupant discovered to be none other than Senator Voltz. "And to think he had ordered his coachman to just drive on, without waiting to find out if she was badly hurt or who she was or anything!" Nora said.

"Dreadful, Mrs. Digby. But why do you put Senator Voltz in that carriage? Why not put some more authentic monster? Hardly anybody drives over women, even the ones they don't like, and you seem to think he didn't even know this one."

"Nobody even knew who she was, and she wasn't able to tell them her name or anything."

"Dreadful," he said again. "And so she was taken to the hospital, and you came on to the party, and Voltz —where did Voltz go?"

"He and the policeman went off together in the carriage—to some nice quiet place where everything could be fixed up, I dare say. I never did think it was anything but an accident, but to just try to sneak out of it like that—"

33

Steele remembered the next morning that Nora had finished her revelations without ever telling him in what way they were supposed especially to concern him—be turned to his advantage was what she had said. It had occurred to him more than once already that Mrs. Digby's vision of the political scene was perhaps not the least of her illusions. He had long suspected her of cherishing among her other fancies the belief that with luck and the indulgence of heaven dueling might be revived; but hitherto the fancies had impressed him as leaning to the absurd rather than the sordid.

He found himself recalling what she had told him because it had been put in a somewhat different light by a paragraph he had read in the *Post* on the way to his office. He wondered if she had seen it. The information that Mrs. Helen E. Davis, regularly employed at the Bureau of Engraving and Printing, had been injured by a fall as she was crossing Pennsylvania Avenue in front of the Treasury the evening before could hardly fail to interest Nora, whether it interested Senator Voltz or not. Witnesses to the accident, the paragraph went on to say, had reported that Mrs. Davis, in stepping out of the way of a passing vehicle,

34

had apparently caught her foot on the edge of the car track and fallen, striking her head on the pavement. It stated further that she had been removed to Dr. McReynold's clinic, where the injury had been diagnosed as a slight concussion attended by severe nervous shock. So Mrs. Digby did not operate exclusively in the abstract, Steele thought, amused. This time she had pulled her rabbit out of what looked like a real hat.

"But you don't have to be afraid Voltz is going to challenge your Richard to a duel, or do anything out in the open; you may rest easy on that score. The man's a coward, Laura; I have my own reasons to know that."

"What reasons, Nora? Has anybody—"

"The evidence of my eyes, for one thing: something I saw him do. I told your husband about it, but of course he is too high-minded to mention it. He is too high-minded to be in politics at all, in my opinion."

"Maybe he thought you imagined it or—something," Laura ventured. The evidence of Nora's eyes might so easily be a figure of speech.

"He pretended to, but he knew better; he had to admit it was true."

"What was it—or can you tell me?"

"Surely I can. But first I want to tell you about the Borinskys' reception. It was undoubtedly the most beautiful one of the season, Laura— Can't you make him do it in a lower key? Or maybe just stop?"

"You know I can't, Nora; not without putting his little night-shade over the cage, and I can't bear to do it on a day like this. Come on in my room; he sounds just loud enough in there."

Laura's room was fresh and fair and full of things, as the bedrooms of ladies in those days were supposed to be. Among billows of dimity and dotted swiss the objects intended for her use were displayed, with others whose intention was for ornament alone and others still that were just too pretty to be used. And there, framed in silver and hand-painted silk, in gilt and ivory, were all her favorite photographs; everywhere she turned, the panorama of her affections confronted her. There were whole rows of Rickie on the walls; in every attitude of pliant infancy he sat and stood and played; he romped with the foxhound puppies by the pincushion on the dressing-table, and under the pink shade of the lamp on Laura's little desk he rode his new velocipede back into that lost October.

Nora sat down in front of the mirror and began to pat her hair. "How do you like it?" she said to Laura in the glass. "The hat, I mean—or had you even noticed it? Cecil always wants me to wear blue, but I tell him anybody can do that.—How darling!"

Not the hat, but Rickie with the puppies. Nora picked up the little picture and held it while she glanced around. "He's everywhere, isn't he? Even without the pictures he is. Do you know, Laura, sometimes when I come into a room where you are, I believe I feel him first."

Laura looked at her.

"As a presence, I mean; as if he were more there than you were. So far there has been no visible manifestation, like the child I told you about, in our apartment in Vienna."

"You didn't, Nora."

"I thought I did; I was telling somebody about it, just recently. It couldn't have been Sabrina—"

"Well, anyhow, what was it? One of those astral things?"

"I don't know what you mean by that, Laura, and I'm sure you don't either. Some day I would like to get your definition of reality. Who was the man—

Newton, Huxley? somebody—who proved things by hitting a piece of rock?"

"Go on and tell me, Nora."

"It was a little boy, about four or five years old I should say, who came quite often, usually when I was there alone but sometimes when there were other people. I would look up from whatever I was doing, or maybe just turn my head, and I would see him: the gayest-looking little chap imaginable, with dark eyes and dimples; he was always smiling. The first time, I thought he must be a child living in one of the other apartments, but the concierge told me there were no children in the house at all. There were only three apartments, one on each floor; it was one of those charming old houses in the Kärntner-Strasse. The concierge had been there twelve years and nobody with a child had lived there in his time, he said."

"And what happened? Did you ever try to say anything to him?"

Nora shook her head. "Never. I wouldn't have done it anyway, but he was never there more than just a minute—just long enough for me to be sure I saw him."

38

"And did he go away—for good, I mean—without your ever finding out anything about him?"

"We went away. We were in Vienna less than a year; it was the shortest station we ever had, and one of the nicest, too. No, I never found out anything about him, and so far as I know he still comes there. I saw him the last time the day before we left. I was putting some things in a trunk, and when I raised my head he was standing at the foot of the bed—you know the kind of carved walnut furniture they have over there—looking at me with that same bright expression. I remember noticing his curls were exactly the color of the polished wood, as if they might have been carved there too."

"But what did you think made him come?"

Nora shrugged her shoulders. "He might have lived there at some time or other for all I know. He might have been looking for somebody; or had something he wanted to say."

"But why to you?"

"To anybody who could hear it. I couldn't, or at least I didn't, but I could see him, and nobody else did even that."

"Could you see how he was dressed?" Laura asked. "You could have told a little by his clothes how long ago it was that he—that he lived there." Her voice was a little wistful. Nora's psychic experiences always interested her, but not this way; she wanted very much to know how the little boy was dressed.

But neither the style nor the material of his costume had made any impression on Nora. "I don't know very much about children's clothes," she explained. "When we were little— But anyhow, I have simply got to tell you about what happened last night at the Borinskys' party." She looked at the small watch that hung looped on a chain around her neck and pinned to the side of her blouse. "Somehow I always get off on these things when I am with you. To me they are the real things. You are a great comfort to me, Laura; I can at least tell you about them."

"You mean even if I don't believe them?"

"Don't understand them; you would have to believe them if you did that."

One of the things Sabrina liked best in Washington was the market. Any housekeeper naturally would, but aside from that, she was sure that nowhere else, not even in Rock Creek Park with all its dogwood and azaleas, did one meet the Maryland spring face to face as one did in the city market. Vegetables should be at least half of anybody's spring; nothing on earth was as flagrantly vernal as some of them were: a young head of lettuce for instance. Even the poets put celery and parsley in their garlands once. Now the new year reviving old desires. Certainly "garden sass" was one of them. But first she always liked to get the roast off her mind. Grace *after* meat.

The things one saw in market, representing as they did an intermediate stage between being alive and being eaten that was almost equally removed from either, had a very unequal effect on the imagination. She had found that out to her sorrow. Legs of lamb no longer skipping in the field and not yet browned with gravy always saddened Sabrina though she had bought so many; as did the tarnished silver of a mackerel when she had it weighed; but how becoming to the cabbages and onions it was to have attained this state, and even to the flowers—washed clean of every imperfection, lifted above the clod! She liked the market in Washington infinitely better than the rich and ragged garden at home where Jake lost his successive battles with blight and bugs all summer long. Fear no more the heat of the sun. She walked down the damp aisles between the brimming stalls, her arms too full already of too many flowers. At home it would be peonies and roses now, but here it was still jonquils and freesias. She was planning to bank them with maidenhair on the marble mantelpiece in the parlor. This time it was going to be a party; there was no way out of it; the Russian Ambassador and Madame Borinsky, with that new attaché and his wife that the Digbys knew so well in St. Petersburg, and the Digbys too, of course; Sabrina counted them off on her fingers; and of course that extra man for her: Captain Webb this time. The company was an improvement, too, on what it would be at home.

Dinner would be earlier there; only the candles lighted and the sky outside still showing pink. The familiar scene came back to her: Laura and the Senator, herself too, and even Jake, in summer white, gleaming like ghosts in the shadowy room; smiling, hospitable ghosts; the huge platter of fried chicken, the silver bowl of strawberry ice cream; and the guests— The food changed a little as the season did: the chickens grew up and got cooked in a different way; strawberries went and peaches came; but the guests were all more or less the same people; not interesting like the ones they had here; not anything especially; just friends. The friends one had at home never seemed to be the kind of people one picked out elsewhere. They had probably never been picked at all. We have our friends, we do not pick them—like the Boston lady: "We do not buy our hats; we have them." Could one never wear one's friends too long?

Laura did not think so. In anything that involved her affections Laura shrank from the very idea of change. To her, going back to the plantation was like going to heaven, almost. She drove in at the gate looking exactly the way she did when she was a bride, and went around perfectly radiant, until she began to realize about Rickie all over again. If she could only have gone on living there forever with just the Senator and Rickie, even without the little brothers and sisters she used to talk about, it would have been one case at least of perfect bliss on earth. I had too much, a star, a sea— And now the little star was gone, and no other little stars in sight, but she still had the sea. Not many women ever had that kind of love given them; certainly not by that kind of man.

Sabrina, walking home with her flowers, wondered if Laura realized all there was to realize about the Senator. She adored him of course and read his speeches and was always afraid something was going to happen to him, but there were currents of which she never seemed to be aware.

The parlor, when Sabrina finished with it, was a triumph. Going into it again, dressed for dinner, she stood in front of the mantel, now fringed with fern and starry with white blossoms, admiring the effect and hoping she was not uneffective herself, in her pale-green dress with her hair so much brighter than it was in the daytime and her freckles showing so much less. Sabrina fair, the Senator called her when he noticed that she had on a new dress, and went on to say the rest of it if he had time—out of *Comus,* where her father had fished up her name:

> *In twisted braids of lilies knitting*
> *The loose train of thy amber-dropping hair—*

Most men were too self-conscious about quoting poetry; they made a sort of joke out of doing it at all; but even Milton sounded quite simple when he repeated it, or Shakespeare. But then, Shakespeare often was. He told her once that he considered Shakespeare and Goethe as two of the most serious of "the doubtful energies in the world," and as a moral force he thought Goethe was perhaps the greater. There were limits in Goethe's philosophy, the Senator said; he prescribed for you: Take, eat. But Shakespeare just gave you everything, as God did, which was a good deal like giving you nothing because you had nothing to compare it with. It made him think of the wine that had been named *Est-Est-Est*. He said that was what you drank when you read Shakespeare.

If he only had more time to talk about those things. Even at the plantation he hardly ever had a minute when people were not coming to see him, about politics or the tenants or the Negroes. Something was always going wrong. "Life is so gay and horrid, Sabrina," he said.

After dinner Madame Doenhof, the wife of the new attaché, wanted Laura to tell her about the South. Everything she had heard about the life down there impressed her as being so much like the way they lived in Russia, she said. In the country, of course; cities were much the same everywhere—did not Laura find? —or were always trying to be. "You must tell me all about your home," she said with her engaging accent. There would be time, she knew. The gentlemen were smoking in the library, and she had learned that in Washington the ladies did not smoke.

"And your so charming husband?" Madame Doenhof's rising inflection persisted even after Laura had complied. "The most brilliant man in your Senate, everyone has called him; he also goes there with you every summer for the—how do you say—*les vacances*? I know so well the happiness of that. And you have children too, perhaps; a home in the country for children—but then too," she amended, hurrying out of the shadow that had fallen, "it is a great *chagrin* when one has to leave them. I say to Nora very often that she is fortunate to have nothing calling to her across any of the oceans in the world. And think of my own good fortune to cross the Atlantic and find her here in Washington!" She put out her hand and took Nora's, lying beside her on the sofa. "We loved always to have her with us in the country, in Russia—"

"And how I loved it too!" Nora said. "There is no other country like it in the world. I always feel that a part of me belongs there. You remember Gogol: 'Russia, what is there between you and me?' I try sometimes to answer that, and I think perhaps it is the sounds more than anything. The voices singing, or only calling to one another in a Russian landscape, are the most haunting thing in the picture. Am I not right, Madame Borinsky? Do you remember this little song we heard so much at Gievko, Irène, on summer evenings?" Nora went over to the piano and found the high, lingering notes she remembered. "You say I have no voices calling; I have those. They are not calling me, to be sure, but I answer them."

"She is completely psychic, that lovely Nora," Madame Doenhof said. "Do you remember the story you told us, Nora, about the Indian who made the rug come downstairs and into the garden? André has never forgotten that story. Tell it to us now."

Nora shook her head. "Everybody has heard it by this time. I do not mean from me, but I believe it has been put in a book. I have even stopped saying I heard it first, though I did: I knew the woman it happened to—or who said it happened; I never altogether believed her. Anyhow, she showed me the rug."

"And she had pulled out some threads from the rug and given them to the man, instead of pulling some of her long gold hairs for him," Madame Doenhof explained, "and so she did not have to do as he wished, and the rug did! Tell something else, then, Nora; *vous avez infiniment de ces histoires.*"

There was time for that too.

"And so," Steele said when they came in not quite too late to hear about the Maharaja's physician who prolonged the lives of his patients by borrowing bits from the lives of other people, "as I understand it, everybody gained and nobody lost by the transaction— provided he really did pay back the time he had borrowed. Are you sure he did, Mrs. Digby?"

"I only know what everyone believed," Nora said. "I did not lend him any; I sometimes wish I had. He only borrowed from the young, you see, and so the days, when they asked to have them back, would be young days, even if they had grown old in the meanwhile."

"But imagine, Nora!" Laura said. "What would anybody want with just a day or two of youth? It would be so useless."

"That depends," Nora said, with her quick smile meeting the eyes of the Ambassador.

"Were the nights included, Mrs. Digby?" he inquired.

48

There are not many words in English whose sound carries for the ear an echo of their meaning; one could wish there were more. On the other hand we have now and then a word that persists in carrying an echo of its own and awakening associations that are entirely at variance with its connotation. For example, remember what we will, the word "Remember" falls sadly on the ear; especially the ears of poets, who are only too ready to seize upon the accident of rhyme to couple it with "December" and "ember" and other melancholy finalities.

Laura would certainly have said it was a sad word: The House Where I was Born, Sweet Alice—there were albums full of such remembering. Nora and her friend Madame Doenhof, however, though most of the things they talked about were in the past, seemed to find them for that reason more amusing. As soon as either of them began a sentence with "Do you remember—" almost invariably they both began to laugh.

"Do you remember the time those poor terrified people from the village came and asked you to hide them in the cellar because there was going to be a pogrom, and then there was no pogrom—"

"And no cherry preserves in the cellar after they

went away—" Madame Doenhof remembered very well. "Seventeen jars, I assure you, Mrs. Steele, they had eaten in their fright, and all cherries; absolutely nothing else; and André laughed so, because they were his favorite too!"

"And do you remember that time when the man was up on the ladder whitewashing the ceiling, and the governess went into the room for something and made him so furious when she told him to be careful where he spit? She had insulted him, Laura. He said: 'Mademoiselle was at least a foot away from where I spit!'"

Laura laughed too, but she didn't believe she would see anything funny in things like that if they happened to her. Imagine the darkies eating up all the preserves! Of course they were not peasants, but she couldn't see how that would make it any easier to put up with. It did not seem to her, as she gathered material for comparisons, that life in Russia was as much like the South as Madame Doenhof had been led to believe. For one thing, at the plantation she and Sabrina were always so terribly busy, and at Gievko, where the Doenhofs' country place was, they seemed to have endless hours every day for nothing but conversation. Not just in th evenings or at meal times, but right in the busiest part of the day.

Laura had never got used to the way Nora visited her friends in the morning; and now Irène—that was Madame Docnhof's name. "And we always find you!" They could not get used to that. Even in Washington, with Sabrina doing most of the housekeeping, Laura still observed the "busy" portions of the day. Her workbasket brimmed with sewing; she whipped miles of ruffles on petticoats for herself and for Sabrina, and featherstitched chemises until it was a wonder they did not fly away with her, Richard said. In Russia nobody sewed, apparently, even with three children. The governess must do that too. But it was lovely to be always so gay.

"One of these days we must have a séance, Nora, like the ones we used to have at Gievko. That poor little table that you made do tricks like a pet poodle! And since then it has not moved except to wax the floor. Did you ever tell Laura about the time you found my bracelet that had been stolen—*Ecoutez donc,* Laura—"

"But why did you think somebody had put it behind the books?" Laura asked after she had listened.

"Couldn't it have just slipped off of your arm some time when you were taking one of them out of the shelf?"

"Because it was the girl herself who was spelling it out when Nora asked her," Madame Doenhof explained. "First of all she spelled her name; it was Antropka; she helped her father in the dairy and came often to the house with the milk, but never to my room. She must have slipped in there some day when we were all away and taken the bracelet; then when everyone was looking for it, she would have grown frightened and hidden it behind the books. It was most strange, Laura. I had quite a—how do you say?—*frisson,* when the table began to tap *Antropka, Antropka,* like that, over and over, there in the almost dark room. And then—what did she say next, Nora?— 'I confess,' *n'est-ce pas?*"

"Yes, 'I confess,'" Nora corroborated. "She said that several times too, and then told us to look behind the books. 'Count three,' she said; you remember we did not know whether she meant three shelves or three books, or whether she was counting from the top or the bottom."

"And it turned out to be all of them!" Madame Do-enhof laughed, the remembered shiver merged in the remembered amusement at the coincidence. "It was the third shelf from the top and the bottom both, Laura, and it was volume three of André's *Histoire de la Révolution française*!"

"And what did you do about it?" Laura asked—"about the girl, I mean. You couldn't accuse her of stealing, could you, without—"

"No, poor thing," Madame Doenhof said. "She had already died in the winter before. This was in the next summer after the bracelet was lost, you see. Nora was just beginning her *rapports* with the spirits. It is wonderful, I assure you, Laura, the things they tell her. When shall we have our séance, Nora? And how, I ask myself, shall we manage without that little table—*qui était si bien apprivoisée*? If I had thought about it, I am sure I would have brought it, strapped together with André's golf and tennis." She laughed again, glancing around Laura's sitting-room for possible substitutes.

"Not here," Nora said with decision; she was glancing at Coq d'Or. "My house would be all right. Some afternoon; night is supposed to be better, but why should it be—in this quiet town? We can draw the curtains."

"And tell your maid it is a Russian lesson we are having," Madame Doenhof said. "She will think that in Russia it is dark, poor girl!"

"And Sabrina might come, Laura," Nora said doubtfully, "if she would promise not to intrude her opinions."

Laura shook her head. "Promising wouldn't do any good."

"No, I suppose not. Between her and your husband I wonder you have any vision at all—any sense of reality."

"But that is exactly what they think, Nora—about my sense of reality. They think it is too easy for me to believe, or to be confused about things that—"

"That they do not want to take the trouble to investigate."

"Not that, Nora, but things that have nothing to do with everyday life—with life in this world, perhaps I mean—"

"But this is not the only world, Laura; everybody knows that. It is not even one of the most enlightened planes of existence. That makes it all the more important to keep as much in touch as we can with higher planes," Nora expounded. "But you come. Would Friday be all right for both of you?"

"What do you three do on Friday afternoons besides worry with the samovar?" Sabrina inquired. "I would just as soon have a steam engine to make tea with as one of those things. And why would anybody want to drink it out of a glass?"

"Because they always do in Russia. They say teacups make it taste strange." Laura smiled. She was willing to admit her own preference for a cup or even for a kettle, but she remained uncommunicative about the Friday afternoons—now gone into the plural; Nora had explained that real freedom in the reciprocal currents could only be gained by establishing a pattern. For some reason—whether the absence of the little table had anything to do with it there was no way of ascertaining—the currents had been disappointingly unreciprocal. But they were picking up.

Sabrina did not pursue the subject. Russian tea, however eccentrically served, was not accountable for the preoccupied look Laura had bent upon her sewing ever since dinner. Nothing was ever needed to account for it; it was the way she sewed.

It was one of their rare evenings without company. They were not even downstairs, but up in Laura's sitting-room, where the yellow tulips in the windows had closed their eyes and Coq d'Or under his nightshade had presumably closed his. The Senator was catching up with the newspapers. Sabrina went back to her book.

"Richard, where did Sam Catesby go after you told him you didn't want him on the High Farm any longer?" Laura suddenly asked.

"I haven't the least idea, Laura. What reminded you of Catesby all of a sudden?" He put down the paper he was reading, with a pile of others on the carpet; this sounded like the beginning of conversation.

"I was just trying to remember some of the people we have had trouble with on the plantation," Laura said. "Of course there always have to be a good many on a place as big as ours, and I was thinking about the way Catesby acted."

"It was bad, wasn't it?" he said. "But we've had a lot of others since Catesby; why do we go back so far —about three years, isn't it? Suppose we consider the

way Luke Mosby behaved last summer—or the way
the Gresham family is going to behave next week
when Murray has the sheriff put them out of the house
they have been loafing in ever since the first of the
year. He says in his letter that is about what he is going
to have to do." It always amused him to have Laura
start a subject this way—exactly like a rabbit. He
wondered sometimes if she herself could tell what
train of suggestion she had followed, as she sat with
that utterly silent work of hers, following it uncon-
sciously too, to all appearances. She hunted in hollows
where the leaves had fallen; she would be there with
out a sound and be gone without a trace; and he could
never follow her because she never led.

"Poor Mr. Murray. I know he must be anxious for
you to come and take some of the responsibility off
his shoulders," Laura said. Then after a pause: "You
never did think Catesby meant to do any of those
things he said he would—to get even with you, you
remember, Richard?"

"Sing, O Goddess, the wrath of Sam Catesby the
scion of— I have no doubt he would have liked to do
every one of them at the moment, but he's had plenty
of time since and hasn't done them yet—that I know

of, at least. What were they, by the way? Was he the one that was going to set fire to the mule barn?"

"That wasn't what Jake told us he said."

"Oh, it was Jake who told us what to expect, was it? In that case I don't wonder you wanted to be sure the curse had been lifted. And speaking of Jake, Murray says in his letter that he saw him cutting the wistaria off of the west porch, presumably by your direction. Murray wanted to be sure you had told him to do it; though of course if you didn't it's too late now. Suppose we don't try to run the plantation from up here in Washington, Laura. Being in two places at once is not a good idea."

"Laura is not in two places," Sabrina said, without raising her eyes from her book. She could nearly always tell what Laura was thinking about for that very reason; she knew just where to look. Those subjects that seemed to be so far afield were usually only a very little way from where Laura was all the time; Sabrina knew that much better than the Senator did. And yet the sudden entrance of Catesby had surprised her too; she found herself wondering, not what had happened to make Laura remember him, since nothing ever had to happen to make her remember anything at home, but why she should have begun to be afraid of him all over again. Could she have been talking to Nora about her past fears as well as her present ones, this afternoon over their tea? Nobody's fears, in Sabrina's opinion, were likely to be lessened by telling them to Nora. She liked to influence people, and it was always easier to do that if they were afraid of something. Nora would go to any amount of trouble, or any amount of kindness either, to get hold of people. Not just because she liked them, though she did that too; she seemed to like almost everybody; she was sweet; but what she really wanted was for them to like her, in a special way that would make her feel important—as if she had a hand in their destiny. Sabrina had known that all along without knowing how she knew it. That was why she was so interested in politics; Nora would learn the *Congressional Record* by heart if she believed it would make the Senator talk to her about what she called political issues, and maybe ask her advice about his speeches. That was why she was so excited over finding out something he could use against Senator Voltz—if anybody could believe it really happened in the first place. Anybody besides Laura, of course; she could always get Laura stirred up. What she was probably doing now was leading her on to talk about some of the other enemies the Senator had made; Laura called them that whether they were political opponents or just sharecroppers; they were the only thing she seemed to be really afraid of. She wasn't a coward; she wasn't even timid the way most women were, about herself. It was just where her affections were involved: the Senator, and of course it used to be Rickie. For some reason Sabrina found herself thinking again of Catesby. What was it he had told Jake he would do to "get even"? Could that have had anything to do with Rickie? Anyhow, whatever it was, she would have to find it out for herself; certainly she was not going to ask Laura.

The blue brocade curtains of the three windows opening on the street were closely drawn against the spring afternoon, but the vertical slits of sunlight persisted. Every single Friday since the séances began had been a lovely day and for that reason difficult to exclude from Nora's drawing-room.

"Maybe the library would be better," she said. "I would have chosen it in the first place except that

Cecil sometimes comes home early and wants a book or something."

"But the last time we had no trouble in here, Nora," Madame Doenhof said. "Maybe it is not the room, don't you think?"

Nora did not reply. With eyes accustomed to the obscurity she looked across at Laura sitting on the other side of the table, her hands still lying palms down on its polished surface.

"But you know I mean to be receptive, Nora," Laura said.

"And yet you make it difficult for him every time. There is always that doubt in your mind. It is hard enough for them to communicate with us even when we do our part; you have no idea what obstacles there are between their state and ours. And then when he has overcome them and reaches you at last—his own mother—imagine the disappointment!"

"But how can I be sure, Nora? The only real message we have had was the one last Friday and it said only those two words—'remember' and 'revenge'— and I have been trying to think of everything I can to connect them with."

"And have you thought of nothing?"

"I can't be sure about that either," Laura said; "but the real trouble is that I cannot connect them with Rickie. I don't believe he would have used those words; I am sure he didn't know 'revenge.'"

"But three years have passed since then, Laura, and besides, their knowledge is different from ours. It might be better if we could make our questions direct; if we asked, 'Was it thus and so?' or 'Was this and that the truth?'"

"Yes, Laura," Madame Doenhof agreed. "Suppose instead of asking what it was that happened, and what made him go without you that day, you could say what in your own mind you believe to be the truth, and he could answer yes or no."

Laura answered neither. She took her hands off the table, as the others had already done, and clasped them in her lap.

"It is a great disappointment to me, Laura," Nora said. "I had so set my heart on being able to help you. I have realized almost from the first day I met you how you were torn continually by this uncertainty, this ignorance. It keeps your sorrow always before you—not to know the truth."

"But let us not give up, Nora!" Madame Doenhof exclaimed. "I had no idea you would give up so soon. Come, let us be very quiet again, and put our hands back—"

The gilt clock on the mantel could be heard now, audibly recording the silent withdrawal of the sunlight from the three front windows. It was some time before there was any other sound in the room. Then quite suddenly the table gave its preliminary raps, and Nora's low voice asked the preliminary question: "Who is there?"

This time, however, the answer was not, as they expected it to be, a name. Instead, the table embarked immediately upon a sentence. "L-o-o-k," Nora interpreted, "w-h-a-t—" Almost as fast as she could supply the corresponding letters the light signals continued, with barely a perceptible pause to mark the ending of each of the eight words the "message" contained; after which display of energy, like a clock that runs down, the table refused to be any longer intelligible and finally stopped entirely.

Nora put the words together: "Look what a beautiful magic Mattie has made," she said, somewhat apologetically. "I can't make anything else out of it; does it mean anything to you, Laura? Was there somebody named Mattie—"

Laura told her; it took some time to do it, with all the little things, such as the quilt scraps, and the witch, and the remembered colors of the autumn woods, and they both looked at her enthralled. Never had they seen her so animated; her cheeks were actually pink—

"But you do believe it now, Laura? No one else could possibly have known those words," Nora said, when the light had been let in and the steam from the samovar was rising. "And you must drink your tea," she urged solicitously. "It is always a shock when one realizes—"

"But a joyful shock, do you not find?" Madame Doenhof's blue eyes were full of sympathy. "It is almost to have the loved one restored, *n'est-ce pas?*" She reached for Laura's hand and pressed it gently with her pretty rings.

Laura returned the friendly pressure and drank her tea, but she was not conscious of the emotions she was being credited with; not all of them. The shock had not been quite what Nora thought and she didn't believe she was feeling the reassurance Irène seemed to be taking for granted. It was all very mysterious, and it must prove something, she was sure of that, but not at all sure that it was anything about heaven and immortality, which had been proved already, Laura thought; that was what religion was for. She knew her Bible very well and had almost learned the eighth chapter of Romans by heart since Rickie died. *For that which a man seeth, why doth he yet hope for?*— She did not have to see, or to hear either, to believe what she knew was true. It was a different kind of hope that the afternoon's experience had given her; she had a warm, almost a happy feeling that maybe the years piling up between her and Rickie didn't count for so much after all. Having those familiar words come back to her, even without their familiar sound, even in that really absurd way, might be a proof of the very thing she wanted most to know: that somewhere there was still a memory of what had happened, a memory that could be put into words again and maybe tell her the things she had felt it so unbearable not to know.

Her mind was busy with this idea while Nora developed her own theories and Madame Doenhof agreed with them. The current was now established, there could be no doubt of that, though Nora thought it might still be intermittent for a while. What Laura must do now was to formulate as clearly as she could the various suggestions that would undoubtedly present themselves to her as having a possible connection with what had happened on that October afternoon. "For you know, Laura, that everything must have an explanation; it is only a question of knowing the facts. And since we cannot know all of them, we must limit our questions. Remember that we are drawing from an unlimited source with only a very small bucket."

Nora seemed quite happy to have found this illustration of the conditions under which they were working; she gave it to Laura to take with her as she said good-by. The afternoon had turned out so much better than she had feared. When Laura glanced back at the drawing-room windows before she turned the corner of the street, Nora was still standing there, waiting to throw her a kiss.

It was Steele's habit to walk to his office every day that he did not have to carry an umbrella. In his opinion, the street was the best of all available places for him to do his thinking. He didn't believe in the idea of stopping to think, or sitting to think. Man was a moving animal living in a moving world, and since his eyes and his mind were moving too, he had no more business stopping to think than he had stopping to stare. The expression "sit and think" had always amused him, he said, because it called up the picture of everybody doing it together—a whole assembly of Rodin's Thinkers all gnawing away on their separate ideas. Bologna's Mercury, caught in the act of leaving the subject after touching it with one toe, would make a better *Penseur* any day than that poor old anthropoid. Streets, rivers, windy places were what helped a man to think.

"Did you ever notice, Sabrina, how little the static aspects of humanity seem to appeal to the great artists? They want their man moving—unless they catch him first and chain him to a rock or set the world on his shoulders, so they can show him wanting to move. And as a figure in history he is naturally on the move; in time, which presumably gets out of his way as he comes on, or in space, which occasionally makes a stand. Who goes there? Could there be a more perfect challenge for the human race? And the countersign— *Pur si muove? Panta rhei?*—And now with your permission I will be flowing too, in the direction of the Capitol."

It seemed to Sabrina that Laura missed a great deal by not coming down to breakfast, which was really a lovely meal, with waffles, and home-cured ham from the plantation, and the heavenly coffee that she had taught the cook not only how to make but how to make the same every day. The dining-room was prettier, or she liked it better, than the one at home; smaller, of course, but ever so much more cheerful, with a glass door opening on a little porch that led down into a sort of garden, mostly ivy, but green all the winter.

The Senator never read his newspaper while he ate his breakfast, the way men were supposed to do; the way her father had always done—looking up every now and then to throw her a crumb of news: "I see where so-and-so says something-or-other." The paper was there by his plate, but he seldom picked it up until he was ready to go. They really had delightful conversations at breakfast. Even this morning, when she was sure he was still thinking about what had happened last night, he did not even mention it again.

Last night Laura had finally told them about the

séances. Not everything, but enough for Sabrina to see
what Nora was up to, whether the Senator did or not.
"I do not believe she is trying to deceive you—no more
at least than she deceives herself," he had told Laura.
But Nora was not deceiving herself just for the sake
of the experience; she was doing the whole thing to
make Laura think of her as a sort of oracle. It would
never occur to him that Nora would want to do that,
because he couldn't see any reason why she should.
Men were actually stupid about some things; even
brilliant men.

But when it came to explaining just how Nora
worked the thing, that was something nobody could
do; at least not so it would convince someone who
wanted to believe it was spirits. Nobody could deny
that it was mysterious—and probably harmless in most
cases. The trouble in this case was Laura's determination to make something out of the "communications,"
as she called them—something definite. What she had
told them last night sounded as if she and Nora were
trying to find somebody to blame for Rickie's death—
or at least for his going off without her that afternoon.
It would be a shame for her to begin tormenting herself about that. It would be a cruel thing for Nora to

make her believe the Senator's enemies might have had something to do with Rickie's being drowned.

Coq d'Or was singing in the sunshine when Sabrina went upstairs. Through the open door into Laura's room she could see her writing at her desk. She could see the picture of Rickie on his velocipede too, because she knew it was there. "Lovely morning," she called.

Laura left her letters and joined her in the sitting-room. How pretty she was, Sabrina thought, in her white dress with all those piles of dark hair. She looked well too; maybe it didn't hurt her after all to be dabbling in this queer business.

"I'm going to town," Sabrina said; "to market, and then shopping. Want anything?"

Laura began rummaging in her work basket. "If you can match this I'd like two more yards," she said; "and if you could take my letter—I won't be a minute—"

"No hurry," Sabrina said.

"I was writing to Mattie; there is something I want to ask her," Laura said, going back to her desk.

Dear Miss Laura—Jake and me cant neither one o us remember if Mr. Catesby came by the house tha

day or not. Nom we didnt neither one of us never see
him talkin to Ricky in the yard after Mr. Richard tole
him to git offn the Hi farm. There dont nobody know
ef hes still somewheres aroun here or not we dont
never see him. Hopin this fine you and Mr. Richard
and Miss Sabrina well and doin well and we goin to
see you soon. From yours truly Mattie D Edmons.

The letter, written large in pencil, lay open on
Laura's desk, so that Steele, coming behind her and
bending down to touch his lips to her hair, read its
contents almost at a glance. He put his fingers under
her chin and turned her eyes up to meet his own.

"I thought maybe—" she began.

"After three years, Laura? And what would it be
worth—what was it worth—to question them, even
the first day?"

"I know, Richard; but then we had so little to
go on."

"And now you have more? Do you believe that,
Laura? Would you be willing to let yourself be guided
by any information you obtained this way—through
following Nora's suggestions?"

"But what do you want me to believe, then, Richard?" The eyes looking up at him were full of tears. "Not the people that were there, and not—"

He drew her away from the desk to sit by him on the sofa. "Now tell me what it was that started you to thinking Catesby had anything to do with this. What was it he said, if you can remember? I mean by that what was it that Jake said that he said? You know what they are like, Laura, all the Catesbys and the Jakes. Was it anything about Rickie? It seemed to me that he had a nice way with Rickie—that he was even nice with his own children; five of them, were there, or six? Mrs. Catesby was the one who used to do battle with them. Poor woman! Imagine six children, or even five, in a house that size—"

"But that was what he said, Richard—don't you remember? That you let them all live like pigs, and that a poor man didn't have any more chance with you than a sinner had with 'God a'mighty,' was what he said, and that he was going to 'level things up yet,' because you were not there all the time, but what belonged to you was and he could wait. And Jake said—"

"Laura! How can you remember all those things? Have you been thinking about them all this time?"

She shook her head. "But I do remember, and now

the messages say things that make me wonder—that
make me—"

"What kind of things?"

"They say that Rickie—Nora believes it is Rickie
who says it, but I don't believe that; most of the time
it doesn't sound a bit like him; I only believe it is something that knows about what happened, and it says
somebody made him go away like that, and —"

Very gently he laid his fingers on her lips. "It is
beginning to seem very strange to me, Laura, that you
who are so lovely in every way should have under-
taken this thing, if only for the reason that it is not
lovely. I would like to have you look at it from that
standpoint, leaving out the question of truth or falsity,
or any explanation of psychic messages and the rest.
Put your head here, while I talk to you. Death is so
large a part of life, Laura; sooner or later it has to be
met by everything that lives. There is no other guest
that comes so often or demands so much—whatever
in the way of a welcome we have prepared ourselves to
give. Tears with the rest; that may be why we have
them; I have never told you not to cry your beautiful
eyes out, you know that. Have your grief, my darling,
forever if you must, but have it whole. That is death's

privilege—that it can stay whole. It is the only thing that does not have to change. Can't you see what a pity it is for you to be chipping and chiseling at it this way—trying to improve a finished marble?"

She lifted her head from his shoulder, so she could shake it, so she could tell him that he did not understand. "I am not trying to change anything at all, Richard, really I am not. I am not rebellious any more, the way I was at first. I believe I am even beginning to be reconciled to giving him up, because I can think of him as being—safer there. I am only trying to understand better about what happened before—about what made it all happen; and that is something that has to do with life, and not with death at all."

He held her hand in his while she finished all she had to say, looking at him with earnestness and hope. Surely he could see—she kept saying, until, raising her fingers to his lips, he told her that he saw.

"It worries me a little," he said, talking to Sabrina about Mattie's letter. "Not that I think Laura is likely to go on with her psychic experiments very long; hardly anybody ever does that. After all, it takes some work and a good deal of concentration, and even i she has the time for it, Mrs. Digby hasn't; but in the meanwhile Jake and Mattie and the others down there can do a little concentrating too. And to think of a girl who knows them the way Laura does being willing to suspend all her knowledge and experience at the suggestion of somebody, or something, that she knows nothing about at all! That to me is the queerest thing about the whole business."

"How do you think it would do to talk to Nora?" Sabrina said. "For me to talk to her, I mean." Certainly the last thing she wanted was for him to do it, for the very reason that she was sure it was the thing Nora wanted most. If Nora could get things to the point where the Senator would be coming to her for advice!

He shook his head. "Laura is not a child, Sabrina. I knew that when I asked her to marry me. We must leave grown people free."

"But Nora isn't leaving her free! And anyhow, nobody ever is free. I've heard you say that; you said it seemed to you that people couldn't rest until they had sold their souls to something—like Faust, you said."

"Then we must leave them at least the freedom of choosing the one they want to sell to," he said, smiling at her. "And we mustn't worry too much, or too soon; not before we know a little better what it amounts to. And by that time we will probably be leaving the astral plane behind us anyhow and getting back to the Delta; a very low plane indeed I should imagine, by Mrs. Digby's standard, or even by mine."

II The Senator

WASHINGTON in those more tranquil years is remembered still by a few people to have had an autumnal awakening that was full of charm. No other Southern town shook off the summer with that expectant breath; no metropolis anywhere in the country looked toward the winter with interest so renewed. Hopes of many colors blossomed in the autumn much as the tulips did in spring; not exalted hopes by any means, nor, perhaps, except in the case of office-seekers, very well defined, but somehow conducive to the state of mind habitually spoken of as atmosphere: a mingling of memory and expectation that in this particular place went well with the soft fulfillment of the Maryland landscape, then so much less withdrawn than it is now. Those illuminated hills and streams have since been bridged and built upon to an optimistic extent that goes only with certainty, which is for some reason less "atmospheric" than the doubts or even the ignorance of that rapidly receding past.

The elms and the beeches around the nursery statue were already golden in October, a month that in the Delta was still overlaid with dust. The trip up had been the dustiest one Sabrina could remember. The cotton fields that ran for miles beside the train as if they were determined not to be left behind were so white with it that you couldn't tell the bolls from the leaves. It was a splendid year for cotton, everybody said—since cotton seemed to like whatever was most disagreeable to everybody else. Even Laura had to admit the summer had been too hot. Her appetite was better already, and she had been back only a week. And after only a week the house on H Street was already shining. Looking out through clear windows on the trees in Lafayette Square, Sabrina too looked out on hope.

The summer had been too hot, and what was more, almost everything that happened had been slightly depressing. More than the usual number of their friends had been away—which Laura, at least considered a drawback—and part of the time Matti had been sick. She had sent her niece to work in he place, and while Silkie was a good girl and a fairly good cook, she was not Mattie. Especially when it came to canning and preserving. And it always did come to canning and preserving, whether there was anybody to do it or not. Laura would do it herself, no matter how hot it was or how she was feeling, rather than let things go to waste. She looked fragile and poetic, but Laura was really tough; anybody who lived on a plantation these days had better be tough. The only thing Sabrina could remember ever hearing her complain of was not being able to sleep, and she hadn't even said any more about that this summer than usual. The main difference they had noticed in her since they left Washington was that she seemed to be less cheerful than she usually was as soon as she turned her face toward home. They might have thought it was because she missed the séances, except that they had already been pretty well given up before they came away. The Digbys were leaving too, and Madame Doenhof. No more spirits, no more samovar, until they all got back in the fall.

The abandonment of these exercises had not, however, made it possible for Steele to judge how far their claim on Laura's interest had diminished. Still, he noted with satisfaction that since coming home she had apparently given up the idea of questioning the servants, which had so astonished him in Washington. Nothing, it seemed to him, could have been less like her than to embark on the uncertainties of that correspondence, and he hoped very much she wasn't going to tackle them orally either; though of course it was possible she had merely postponed her intention until she got the preserving done. He was himself too incessantly harassed by the accumulation of political and agrarian matters that he found stored up for him, to be as attentive as usual to the lights and shadows of the domestic scene—besides being very often absent from the scene.

"Guess who I saw down there at Sherwood," he asked one evening at dinner, as if the thought had just occurred to him. "An old friend of ours, and I'll give you twenty guesses, ten apiece. I'll give myself a handicap too, by telling you the color in advance: white."

Old friends, even white ones, were numerous enough to keep the game open while Jake changed the plates and brought in the lemon pie—not without one or two suggestions of his own.

"Very well, then; you're getting cold, so I'll have to tell you. A tenant farmer by the name of Catesby, now tilling the Sherwood acres and, from what I gathered, doing it no better than he did on ours."

"I hope his behavior is better," Sabrina said, accepting her pie. "Did you tell Mr. Osborne about him?"

He shook his head. "I thought I would just let Osborne tell me. I believe he has been having a pretty bad time of it down there. Malaria. He lost two of his children with it, Osborne says, and his wife has been sick for the last year."

"Did you say anything to him, Richard?" Laura asked. "To Catesby, I mean."

"Not very much; we were in a hurry; riding back from town and late of course. He was out at the gate as we passed his house. He sent you a message—or you can take it as a message. He said his wife had never forgotten how good you had been to them, especially the children. Do you know, Laura, I believe Silkie is better than Mattie on lemon pie. Or maybe it's just the appetite that riding makes."

On the porch in the late evening after the moon came up, there was always a breeze. It seemed to Laura to come with the moon, but that was because she could see then that the leaves were moving. "Isn't it heavenly to see the coolness as well as feel it, after a day like this?" she said, breaking a silence that had fallen. "And Sabrina upstairs where it's so hot, in bed with a book!" The silence fell again.

"I am so sorry about the Catesbys, Richard," she said after a while. "Even before you told me that at dinner—ever since we came home I have been realizing that maybe I was all wrong; that it would be dreadful to think anybody could be so wicked, unless I really knew it was true."

"Thinking people are so wicked is nearly always a little risky, isn't it? Even when we have our proofs lined up, we can never be sure that all the returns are in. Some outlying district in the critter's soul may still have a vote. But I'm glad you see that this time you hardly had a case to start with."

"I know," she said, "and I'm beginning to feel so unhappy to think I put Rickie into it that way—into my suspicions, I mean. I was trying to see all that evil through his precious eyes, that were so blue and innocent, Richard—"

"There, there—" he stopped her. "Suppose we don't do any more accusing. Not you, and not ever

Nora. There are outlying districts in Mrs. Digby's soul that never will be heard from, I imagine: wild Irish regions—or Indian, maybe. She is a queer friend for you to have annexed, Laura—or to have annexed you. I can't get used to it."

Madame Doenhof adored Washington more than ever after being away from it for three months. Seated next to Steele at dinner, she could not find, in an idiom unimproved by her Newport summer, enough agreeable things to say to him about his so charming little capital. She was continually intrigued by its so feminine charm. "It is altogether like the women of your country, do you not find, and not in the least like your men?"

He would have to think that over, he said, not ever having thought of it before. "It might help me, though, if you would tell me just what opinion you have formed of the women of my country since you have been in it. We will leave out the men, since they have not left their mark anywhere around, and just take the ladies."

"They are charming."

"Washington, then, is charming."

"I find it so, very much. But—you will pardon me—I find it also less chic than European capitals."

"And the ladies too, less chic?"

She nodded. "But still they have elegance; and your city too has that—*une élégance tout à fait spéciale, vous savez*. It is that which interests me. It is as if one had arrived there by a stroke—how do you say?—*un coup. On a sauté le ton pour arriver tout d'un coup à l' élégance*."

"Delightful," he said; "and rather surprising. I thought that right now my countrywomen were less concerned with the fine points of civilization than with a pretty rugged determination to get what they call their rights: votes and things."

Madame Doenhof shrugged her very white shoulders. "Your women are free beyond belief," she said.

"But not beyond faith, hope, and imagination. Belief is, I am afraid, only a small spark of the sustaining spirit by which they operate. They want to be very free indeed, you see."

"But not the women of your South—not Laura, *par exemple,* who would never care for votes at all? She is always to me so far from politics; so unlike to Nora, who must be taking part in some question wherever she is. In Russia she was so—*tellement révolution-naire* that for her husband, and also for André, it was many times a little difficult. And here too—she has told you perhaps about the happening at the reception given by your President to the Americans of the South—*Le Congrès Pan-Américain?* You were not there; you should have been; she must tell you.—Nora!"

Nora, across the table, shook her head. "Cecil told me to shut up about it," she said.

"But he knew you would not shut up; *n'est-ce pas,* Cecil? And surely with us here—so *intimes,* so understanding—" She glanced around her own small dining-room.

"Quite," the Honorable Cecil agreed, directing his monocle to the guests from the Delta in turn. "So hand-picked, I should say, for a tirade on the race question."

"But it is not that at all, Cecil," Nora broke in. "It is a point of etiquette pure and simple. The question is merely this," she went on, addressing the intimate and understanding others: "Should Mademoiselle Légitime be asked to a ball and not be asked to dance? And that is not a race question until someone chooses to make it so; which is precisely what I am objecting to."

"Mademoiselle Légitime?" Steele asked.—"Oh yes; from Haiti."

"The daughter of the ex-President," Nora said. "Quite a pretty girl, charmingly educated, exquisite French, exquisite gown; and permitted to sit through the entire evening without being invited to dance— or to do anything, for that matter; she went in to dinner with her own father, if you please; a thing that could not happen in any other capital in the world. Personally, I should call it a national disgrace. Somebody should have gone to your President about it, or to your Secretary of State. I tried to make Cecil go—"

"But he funked it," Steele said sympathetically. "We all know Cecil, Mrs. Digby."

Count Doenhof looked at Laura, amused. "How quickly Mrs. Digby arranges things," he said.

"Don't let them tease you, Nora," Laura said. "I don't think it should have happened either, but I don't believe the President could have done anything about it, or Secretary Owen—or Mr. Digby, even if he had wanted to; not then; it would have had to be done before."

"Before what, Mrs. Steele?" the Honorable Cecil inquired.

"Before the present and beyond the past," Steele quoted. "The trouble, Mrs. Digby, is that you are too young. All these things got started wrong before your time. We will have to get you some new grievances—if we can find such a thing."

Nora, her cause abandoned, gave him her sudden smile. "Could you perhaps invent one?"

He shook his head. "Think a moment what I would run into! Infringement of title, new names for old devices—Worse than the Patent Office."

"Nothing new under the sun," Count Doenhof said. "And that holds for human stupidity as well as human injustice."

"And did it ever strike you, Count André," Steele asked him, "how embarrassing that makes it for the reformers—to be always running into the same misbehavior over again, and not always recognizing it quickly enough? Suppose, for instance, one of them starts blasting away at infidelity in the home, and suddenly realizes that he is giving the most dreadful names to—Francesca and Paolo, say."

"Or Tristan and Isolde," Count André said. "The

poets' darlings would fall pretty generally under the ax, wouldn't they?"

Steele thought a moment. "So far as I can remember right off, they would. It's all very confusing, isn't it, Madame Doenhof?"

Madame Doenhof admitted that it was, a little—in English.

"I will explain it to you, Irène," Nora said. "It is this: Laura's high-minded husband seems to think we can be just as—impetuous as we please, provided we can get a poet to sing about us. He doesn't have to apologize for us, you understand; not in the least; just sing."

"It depends a little on the song, though," Count André suggested.

"That doesn't change the ethics in the least," Nora said. "He's still putting art ahead of morality."

"But can he, if it's bad art?" Steele asked her. "I didn't know you could put anything behind that."

She gave him another smile.

"I never did know why poets couldn't do a better job with good people, Mrs. Digby," he said. "I'm sorry about it myself; it would reconcile a lot of things."

"And I believe they do even worse with just ordinary respectable ones, which is all most of us aspire to be," Count André said. "Still, outside of literature, we much prefer associating with each other than with the good poetic material. There must be plenty of it around—if we ever wanted to look it up."

"Maybe if everybody came out and told the truth about himself we wouldn't have to look," Nora said. "We might try it once in a while, just for a change."

Steele shook his head. "It wouldn't do, though; turning truth over to amateurs is much too dangerous. That is one thing we have got to leave to the artists."

"Then why do you think of it any more, Laura? Why do you not put it out of your mind completely?" Nora left her chair and came over to sit on the chaise-longue by Laura's feet. "You will be surprised to see how quickly it will vanish," she said. "None of the influences that come to us from those higher planes ever insist on remaining; they are meant for a blessing, and not for a burden, and the moment we show them they are unwelcome, they disappear. They are not like human beings, who so often keep on trying to help us even after we show them their efforts are mistaken, or perhaps not understood. Let me think a minute how I can explain it better."

Laura sat up against her pillows, watching her while she thought.

"It is like this," Nora said. "We should not think of this knowledge, this wisdom, as either coming or going, but as staying, as being always here. It is we who come and go. Do you not see that in this way you are completely free to think of what you please? But now, with such a terrible cold, you should not think of anything. And you must not blow your nose like that. Here—" She went over to the dressing-table where Rickie and the puppies stood by the pincushion in their silver frame, and got one of the cut-glass bottles, and a fresh handkerchief from the lace and ribbon sachet.

"But what you say about feeling farther away from him than you did before," she said, sitting down again and dabbing the handkerchief with the bottle, "is totally unreasonable, Laura. If you do not believe the messages were from him, then you do not believe it, and that is all—for you at least. So far as you are concerned, it was something else, or nothing at all. But in either case it could not take him farther away from you; that is nonsense."

"Only in my feeling about it, Nora. And it may be just the contrast—the disappointment—after feeling him so near. Now there are days when I seem to have lost him completely; when it seems as if he is nowhere at all. At home this summer all the places that used to bring him back so—didn't do it any more."

"Don't talk about it now, Laura. Lean back and shut your eyes and let me lay the handkerchief over them. The real trouble is your not sleeping any more than you do. When one lies awake at night and just listens to time going by, what can one do besides imagine things? I am going to bring you something to make you sleep, and after you have had some good nights we will talk about these things again. And another trouble is that you have had no other trouble—which sounds funny, but I mean just that; nothing but this in your whole life, as far back as you can remember, that was not fortunate, is that true? And even if this is the very worst of all, as it may be for a woman—I do not know—still it lets you concentrate too much. Some day I am going to tell you—"

"Tell me what, Nora?"

"And what if you didn't believe me?"

"But I would—you know I would—unless it was something like the mango tree, or that boy in the basket getting cut to pieces with a sword and then coming out alive."

"It was a little like that," Nora said. "At least I did come out alive. You have no idea what the world is like, Laura; how people hate each other. I was born in India because my father—he was a captain in an Irish regiment—hated England and would have fought against the English—or so they pretended. At all events his regiment was one of those they were afraid to keep at home. And in India, there were the English again, and the French and the Germans, all hating one another and hating the Indians too—all the different kinds of Indians, who didn't have to be taught anything about hating because they had their different kinds of religion to teach it to them. Do you know, Laura, sometimes I think the only universal feeling must be hate."

"But that is only among nations, isn't it, and not individuals? And only every now and then, when they have a war, or when they are trying to shift things around so they can avoid having one? And even when that is going on, there are always friends and families who go on loving one another. You can't say it is universal, Nora."

"Friends and families!" Nora said. "It was my father's friend that my mother left her five children to go away with, if you please. And it was her brother, her half-brother he was, her father's illegitimate son, in Ireland, who sold her land and kept the money for himself. Think of it, Laura—robbing her children of every penny, so that it was an outcast and a pauper that Cecil married when he married me! The world is an evil place I tell you, and I have seen more of it now when I am thirty-two than many people have seen when they are dying of old age."

"But you are so gay, Nora! Nobody would ever think of you as having had all that trouble; it hasn't left a scratch on you that anyone can see."

Nora shrugged her shoulders. "And what would they do about it if they did see? They might like to hear such a story once, and then forget right away that they had ever heard it. They have their own sorrows to look at when they feel like being sad. It is because you look at yours too much that I am telling you this about myself."

Laura reached for her hand and stroked it gently. "But you are happy now, aren't you? You are more admired than anybody. You are always being envied for your interesting life, and all the places you have been in."

"And that is another curious thing," Nora said— "the idea people have that one place must be better than another. I suppose that would account for all the moving done in the world; for the railroads and the ships, and even for the first little paths that were made in the forest by bare feet. And do you not imagine if people ever found a perfect happiness in any of those places, that everything would suddenly stop? Because they would be then where they wanted to stay forever. I think for the most of us, Laura, it would just be in somebody's arms." She looked at her watch. "I must be going—always going, you see. But this time it is only into the arms of the dentist, so there is no fear that you have seen the last of me. Be very careful of yourself, Laura darling. Everybody is sad when you behave like this."

The political revival in Washington was less hopeful, even in those hopeful years, than the social one—

through being better understood, no doubt. To Steele, coming back in the fall was perennially depressing. Turning from the agrarian scene, like a sort of reversed Cincinnatus, to any scenery likely to be provided by congressional means, seemed to him the annual turning of a worm. There may not have been much in the Delta to make a man want to live there, but for the first few weeks he could see little in Washington to make him want to live at all. Every year he had to get used to that way of doing business all over again.

Just how confusing would the political processes of a free government be to a student who had not been warned that he must approach the subject with an open—one might even say an empty—mind? Who enters here must leave practically everything behind that might be applicable to any other proceeding under the sun; first and foremost the ordinary usages of speech. The fact that laws were made and the fate of nations decided in words that had apparently lost their relation to the objects they defined seemed to Steele in the beginning an astonishing thing, a willful and unnecessary complication of a business whose very essence was not simple. Gradually, however, he had come to recognize certain advantages in the system. A convention was by nature a convenience, once you got used to it, and who was he to be exacting about the use of words? He could never catch the thing he meant in verbal nets of his own contriving; why not take other meanings in others' words, and not insist on honorable gentlemen being honest or expect a statement defined as true to be anything that you could trust?

Still, he had read somewhere not long ago that man's conscience had been gifted with a voice in order to make him a reliable witness to what went on around him in the universe. No room for conventional meanings there. On those terms his first duty, silence being out of the question, would be to check everything he reported with the universal fact. Some leeway might be allowed to poets, he supposed, but none to politicians. Just what effect would this ruling, if it were taken seriously, and if the thing that conscience had were indeed a voice and not an echo, have on civilization? So much of what we called civilization was verbal anyway.

A large part of his own experience having been among Negroes whose civilization was too thinly imposed to obscure some of the advantages of a different point of view, he had been afforded refreshing glimpses of variety in the handling of moral problems as well as those of a purely practical nature. The darkies in his part of the country had certainly never heard of Mark Twain's injunction to be economical with the truth because it was our most precious possession; yet they were by nature not only extremely cautious themselves in the use of the truth, but naturally expected everybody else to be; and he had noticed that by this consistent line of behavior the truth was sometimes saved among them where the confusion of a more instructed handling might have lost it. He had seen it lost more than once, or lost sight of, in the effort made by white people to do what is called tracking down a lie, or bringing one home—not as a mere preliminary to getting hold of the truth, but as if it were an end in itself—somebody's most precious possession. If he says that I said, then he is. If I am not what he says I am, then what is he?—All the way from the playing fields of schoolboys to the halls of Parliament or the Council of Trent, the chase of the *tu quoque* had been a sport and spectacle of—civilization, he supposed; certainly the primitive mind could be depended on to steer clear of such academic by-paths.

He recalled an occasion at the plantation when he had tried to find out what had become of the letters he had failed to get by the noon mail.

"Jake says he gave them to you, Sam, and asked you to bring them to the house for him. He says you were standing in front of the store when he came out of the post office. That was on Wednesday, you remember."

"I wuzn't at the sto' on Wednesday, Mr. Richard. I ain't been to the sto' nary day this week."

"You hear that, Jake? Sam says he wasn't at the store."

"Yes'r, I heard him."

"Well then, what did you do with the mail?"

"I give it to Sam."

"Where was he when you gave it to him?"

"He was standin' in front of the sto' jes' like I been tellin' you."

That was not the end, but as he remembered it the end was in no way more conclusive. The various lies had all remained at large and nobody's friendship had been sacrificed in the cause of truth. He and Jake and Sam had remained precisely as they were before, both to themselves and to each other—a mystery, as God intended.

Sabrina was beginning to wonder how much longer the Senator could manage to be so serenely unconscious of the way Nora felt about him. It was very commendable of course to see no evil, hear no evil, and speak no evil, like those three little symbolic monkeys, as long as one could afford to ignore such a large part of what was going on, but the question was, with a woman like Nora going on, how long could he afford it? All the women who ever knew him had probably been devoted to him; in a way he must be used to it; but Nora had started this almost before she knew him at all and had gone about it in a way he couldn't possibly be used to. She wasn't an American woman to begin with, and that made all the difference in the world. Sabrina was beginning to wonder if maybe she ought to give him some sort of hint. But he probably wouldn't understand it if she did, and if she came right out in so many words and told him— She tried to imagine what the words would be, and failed: she could only imagine the way he would look at her. He would think she had lost her mind.

He had always thought she was too direct, too out-spoken, about almost everything that came up. "Don't let the stage scenery collapse as long as you can help it." He had told her that lots of times. About her love-affairs even—such as they were.

"But weren't you a little harder than was necessary on the poor boy?" That was Victor Brassant, who had been sitting out on the porch asking her to marry him and refusing to take no for an answer; she thought he never would get on his horse and go home. She was still out there on the steps watching them appear and disappear in the patches of moonlight under the trees, on their way to the gate, when the Senator came out through one of the long windows and sat down by her. "I am sorry, Sabrina, but I heard every word. I knew that if I got up he would see me; I can't imagine why he hadn't seen me in the first place; and you know he didn't give either one of us much warn-ing." He leaned back against the white column be-hind him.

"It doesn't matter. Not to me, at least, and of course he never will know."

"You sound as if you were not very sorry for him."

"I'm not."

"Why not?"

"Well, in the first place, just as I told him—you say you heard me—I had never given him the least right to say those things to me."

He shook his head without taking it from the column; he was looking up at the moon. "Suppose you could not give him the right—nor withhold it either? Suppose he inherited it, from Adam we'll say, though we could go back a lot further. It's almost the oldest title in a man's possession, the way I look at it. But leaving out his side of it, don't you think for your own sake you shouldn't have handled him quite that way? Next time you might try Belinda's technique. You remember Alexander Pope's Belinda? The lady who lost her lock?—

Favors to none, to all she smiles extends;
Oft she rejects, but never once offends.

Next time I'd like to see the poor fellow with something to hold him up on his way home besides just his horse. He's a nice boy too, Victor. I always liked Victor." He sat there looking down the drive where Victor had disappeared.

Sabrina had often thought about that summer night. She had not been called upon to remember Belinda's technique very much, but she had tried to improve her own methods and not be quite so efficient in the way she handled things. The fact remained, though, that something ought to be done about Nora. She was upstairs in Laura's sitting-room right now, talking about goodness knows what. What topic had succeeded spirits, she wondered—politics again, or just the Senator? Today she had come as usual with a rose for Laura—that rose for Laura's writing-desk they were all used to—but this morning there was something else: a bunch of peppergrass for Coq d'Or. Even a canary ought to be able to see through that.

"Will you give it to him, Laura, or shall I? To make him sing, the man at the bird store said. 'And what do you have to make him hush?' I asked him, and you should have seen the way he looked at me! More disapproving even than you, Sabrina. 'Who wants to make him hush?' he said, like that. You can imagine how I hung my head. One is always ashamed of not liking what is gay, even if it is only a gay noise. Morning's at seven, God's in his heaven—I used to know that song. I made gay noises once myself. Look at him, both of you! He does like it! I didn't really think he would. Sing then, you little Pippa Passes!"

"Do you know what I'd like to do, Sabrina—once anyway? I'd like to go straight up to an object, either a person or a thing, and assert or deny something about it as a fact, without feeling obliged to walk all around it and find out what was behind it and what it was standing on and how it happened to be there, and maybe end up by wondering if it really was there. And the Lord God brought them to Adam to see what he would call them. Think of being able to say 'elephant' right off and be perfectly sure you were right!"

"My, but you're silly," Sabrina said.

"I wonder if I am. I wouldn't like to be too sure of even that apparent fact. It's a bad idea for anybody who makes a living out of politics to start toying with shades and nuances. His business is with the primary colors—all the violent and insubordinate contrasts, all the platitudes. There is a lot of strength in a platitude, any platitude, or it never would have lived long enough to be one, and I don't suppose there ever was one that had outlived its usefulness. That's an interesting thing to work on—the average life-span of the platitude. We don't have to specify the language, since there seem to be no barriers of that nature that they can't fly over like a bird."

"Are you still wondering?" Sabrina asked him.

"Still wondering, but going. I haven't got a very nice day ahead of me, with that food bill of mine. And it looks as if it might rain. Daring me to leave my umbrella, I suppose."

It did rain. The gallery was almost empty of visitors in the afternoon when Steele finished with his bill, which seemed to him pretty empty too, and turned to leave the floor. As he went to the cloakroom a page met him with a note. It said: "I have your umbrella. Will give it to you at the west door. Nora."

"I told Laura I was coming and she asked me to bring it; but it has stopped raining," she said, handing him his property.

"It may begin again. Do you want to try walking? Having an umbrella will not help the puddles, you know."

"Surely I will be walking," she said, giving him her quick smile; "and talking too. I never seemed to get the chance for it I have been wanting. I planned this some time ago."

Nora was not tall; her head came no higher than his shoulder; but she had an easy stride that kept her step even with his. The hat she wore would not seem rational for a rainy day or indeed for any kind of day at the present time, but the blue cape swinging from her shoulders, having the same intention of shedding the water that a tent or a roof might have, had much the same enduring grace of line. The pavement was wet enough to require a reasonable amount of her attention, but the eyes she turned now and then on her companion had taken on, as they often did, an allurement that must have seemed to almost any man a little out of reason, and Steele was afraid the things she was preparing herself to say to him might turn out to be very unreasonable indeed.

"First of all," she said, "I might as well tell you that I cannot understand you any more than if I had never laid eyes on a man before. You get more and more difficult for me all the time."

"Why do you try?" he said. "Understanding anybody takes a lot of work and hardly anybody is worth it."

"Aren't you?"

"Heavens no! And I really am impossible. I have

got myself into a muddle that is too deep even for me. How would you like to just let me try to understand you instead? However little I succeeded, I couldn't miss being repaid."

"Stop right there," she said. "That's exactly what I'm talking about. You say things like that all the time —to women, I mean—and you really despise every one of them, in the sense of looking down on them and feeling yourself superior. You treat us all, even Laura, as if we were the merest children—me the worst of all. Why do you? No, let me finish." She put up her hand to stop him while she collected the thoughts which were apt to come a little behind her words. "When I first met you," she began again a trifle less volubly, "I thought we would be the kind of friends who could help each other, and then of course I saw that nobody would ever be able to help you, because you never need it. I believe you are the only man I ever saw who was really a grown person. Almost all of them have something that has stayed exactly as it was when they were little boys—" She broke off. "Perhaps you never were a little boy," she said, looking at him seriously.

"Perhaps it was only a long time ago."

"Well, at any rate, if there is going to be any helping done, it's you who will have to help me. And God knows I need it. You would never believe how little help I have ever had, from a living soul. That is the reason I keep reaching out and trying to get in touch with something outside of me—something that really can help. It is not just foolishness, as you think it is."

"I am sure it is not," he said. "Not always; not often perhaps. We all need help from whatever source we feel free to call upon. I should be glad to know that you felt free to call on me."

She laid her hand on his arm and they walked for a little while in silence. "Suppose you put up your umbrella," she said; "I think I felt a few drops. Now —that is better; now I can ask you something." But she walked on without doing it.

"Do you believe," she began presently, "can you possibly believe, that it hurts you in any way, or hurts Laura, for me to love you as you must know I do—as I have done almost from the beginning? I think I knew the first time I saw you that you were the only person in the world who could help me—who could teach me the things I have always wanted to know. I have never known what to believe about anything hardly. I could even be good if you would help me, if you wouldn't be always pushing me off as you do—pushing me down. I believe you could save my soul; but if you don't want to, I am just lost, and that is all."

He looked down at her face. "Is it so simple as that?" he said.

She nodded, holding her lip between her teeth, biting back her tears.

"Nora! You say I treat you as if you were a child. I know very well that you are not a child. You are not asking me to save you, but to love you, with all that loving a grown woman means to a man."

"And would it be so hard for you to do?" she said. And when he did not answer: "You are not a saint; I could not love you if you were."

"No, not a saint," he said. "I see you have made out that much about me anyhow. Shall we turn down here?"

"It's the quickest way to get me home, I suppose," she said, but she did not seem to be offended; she did not let go his arm.

They took the other street and walked on without speaking. This time it was he who broke the silence.

"I'll tell you one way I know I used to be a little boy," he said cheerfully, looking down at her. "You've heard of the institution known as the colored mammy? Well, I had one, and I can remember still how she used to make me say my prayers, every night of the world. The idea seemed to be that neither one of us would sleep a wink if I didn't, and so of course I did. And then when we got through, I kneeling and she sitting, she would encourage me to go on and tell the Lord a few things not in the rubric—events of the day in which I had acquitted myself well or ill—and get His opinion, which she was authorized to give. It was all very informal; it was one gen'leman talkin' to another, was the way she put it; and I believe it was good for both of us—me and the Lord, I mean. Even now I can imagine He finds it more entertaining to talk to me than if I were a saint. Just as you say you do." They walked on.

"Here we are," he said at last. "And do get those wet shoes off right away. And thanks again for the umbrella."

On the highly ornamental calendar facing Steele as he sat at his desk, the motto for the current month, gracefully encircled by a wreath of autumn leaves, made the following statement:

> *I am the master of my fate:*
> *I am the captain of my soul.*

He had been reading it automatically for about two weeks now, this being the middle of the month, but today for some reason he put his mind on it. He had often noticed a tendency on the part of the people who made calendars (who were they, by the way?) to set the natural information they conveyed under captions of a spiritual implication. More and more they were becoming vehicles of moral precept. The final word on any ethical question might at this rate come to be finally attached to some day or month of the almanac; which, when you came to think of it, was a curious place for it to be. The pages that record the changes of a turning wheel, the moon's inconstancies and the vagaries of the stars, seemed an impermanent setting for the last judgment or even the last hope of any one of us. Who in the world, seeing it there, could ever think of it as the last?

"On such and such a day, anno Domini so and so, I was (or thought at the time I was) the master of my fate"—the higher criticism would demand something a little like that. Nobody would read it, of course, but nobody read it now either. They did once, probably, before its assumption by the calendar. A poet even wrote it once, not so long ago. It was a red-hot spark from the burning desire we all feel to get things into their ultimate shape——for ourselves, naturally. We may want it for other people too, but by that time it has stopped being poetry.

The passion for stability, for fixation, had begun to seem the greatest of mysteries to Steele. Where did it come from? It was, so far as he could learn, man's own, and up to date his only, original idea—in the sense of *Ursprung*. German was wonderful when it came to words like *Ursprung*.—Imagine a baby born in a shop where every wheel was turning; oily belts moving noiselessly in every direction over his head, the floor revolving on its own axis under his feet—by the time he found them. Imagine him swaying around in a world like that and seeing everybody else swaying too, not only physically but in every other way, growing, changing, fading. Why on earth, if he ever got hold of a pencil and a piece of paper, would he want to write about things standing still? What would give him the idea? And why would he like it so much that he would immediately give it to whatever God he happened to have at the time? With Him is no variableness, neither shadow of turning—even if He was not in the least like the God he had yesterday. And yet, when it came to death, which had so many of those once-and-for-all attributes—

How strange it was, he thought, that here where we see rest for the first time, we are for some reason always in a hurry. Do not wake me; do not ever wake me—yet that is the thing we try to do.

Very well, then, I am the captain of my soul. With no nautical training whatever I find myself on the bridge of a ship—and such a ship! Nothing turned out of any shipyard that ever existed: an heirloom vessel, patched and mended and repainted goodness knows how many times. When I think about the wonders and the terrors of the voyages it has had already, I feel less like a captain than ever. I feel like the ancient mariner, wearing my doom around my neck, more absorbed in the perils of the scenery than in any probable destination—the perils and the enchantments—

—where coral reefs lie bare
And the cold sea-maids rise to sun their
streaming hair.

And to sing, naturally. None of the poets has ever said what about. The idea seems to be that they are holding out enchanting promises. Maybe they are only asking to be taken on board. Save me!

"Nora seems to be unhappy over something, Richard, have you noticed? Of course she has had enough unhappiness in her life to keep her from ever being anything else, but the most wonderful thing about her is the way she almost always manages to be gay. She says she does not want to add her sorrows to the load the world is carrying already. She is really very unselfish in spite of being spoiled—if she is spoiled. Sabrina thinks she is; she thinks she has had too much admiration. But she has had all those other things too. I never heard of a family like hers, Richard. They did the wildest things and got into all kinds of trouble, and she says at least one in every generation committed suicide on account of some love-affair. They were fated to do it, Nora says—like the race of Asra.

Do you know that poem? Nora said it was one of Heine's—

> *Mine is the race of Asra*
> *Who perish when they love.*

That is all I can remember of it. She says it is beautiful in German."

Not everybody came to Washington in those days. Our contemporary claim that by standing in the Union Station or at the foot of the Washington Monument and exercising a little patience we can see everybody we ever heard of, had not been made at that time. The Union Station, indeed, had not yet been built, and though the Monument had been at last completed, the dream of such unlimited social advantages had probably not begun. The fact that some people did not come, however, may have made it nicer in many ways for those who did, whether one had ever heard of them or not, and certainly made it more reasonable for them to linger. Steele had encountered, not in the usual haunts of sightseers, but unexpectedly none the less, more than one friend of his student years abroad whom business or pleasure had brought to Washington. Augustus Silvain, of whom many had heard since those days in Aachen, had dropped in one morning—from no nearer than Aachen, so far as Steele's knowledge of his movements went—to tell him he was engaged in designing some of the neo-classic embellishments of the capital.

"I had no idea it was to be politics," he said, glancing around Steele's office. "Literature would have been my guess; I don't remember that I quite put you down for poetry."

"I had already been put down for making a living before you ever saw me," Steele said.

That was all, on the subject, and what a satisfaction it was, he thought, to let it go at that—their common past, that segment of experience they had accidentally shared—and not be invited to run about the bracs and pu' the gowans fine. How fine would they look to either one of them, pressed by this weight of years? He had liked Silvain well enough in those days; might be said to have picked him in fact; but suppose he met him now as he was then—"Lord! Suppose I met myself, mooning around the university, and had to listen to some of the opinions I held then! *Resurgam*. But which one of me? Not the young collegian on this occasion at least, thank goodness."

The subject when they met was apt to be art, whose own resurgence along special lines then taking place in Washington rather defied the philosophy of artists. So startling a product of the Western Hemisphere might not, they thought, feel at home there, even on a scale that was vast enough to bring conviction with it.

"How long do you artists give your creations to become 'indigenous'?" Steele inquired. "I suppose it depends on popularity rather than on mass."

"More on history—or the lack of it; on ignorance generally, I should say."

"A friend of mine used to maintain that ignorance was good for some things, and art was one of them. He did not speak from the creative standpoint; he was not an artist himself; an appreciator, and something of a collector. I suppose in that line his ignorance had cost him less than his knowledge."

"Insisted on applying it, no doubt; that's the trouble with knowledge. That's why ignorance is so restful; it makes it possible to let things alone."

"An enlightened ignorance might—knowing that he knows not. It wouldn't be restful long, though. Ignorance doesn't know enough to stay ignorant. But after all, rest is not the great objective. In this country at least we're supposed to be pursuing happiness."

"Defined as—?"

"Everybody has his own definition, naturally. Free country."

"Yours, then?"

"Mine—oh, something too indefinite to be defined at all, I suppose; just pursued; the end of the rainbow. As soon as you begin to talk about it you find you are talking about something else. Nice of you not to put me down for a poet. I would always have found myself talking about something else, I'm afraid."

Silvain looked at him. "I should imagine most Americans could manage a more concrete presentment of what they were after than that," he said.

"Probably; but not necessarily more permanent. Naming the thing doesn't make it what they think it is; doesn't keep them from being off after something else equally concrete."

"Well, as a purveyor of the concrete I like to encourage the idea that happiness is architecturally obtainable. Besides which, I believe in setting up something to commemorate the politicians and the millionaires who, whatever else they may have done, at least made building possible. That's a good deal, when you stop to think about it; it's most of Rome. It's a lot of Venice too. The purists in architecture can still criticize them, if they want to be so pure, and let you people alone."

"It's a funny thing," Steele said presently, "that the really indigenous thing about art in this country is its aspiration after just this classical ideal that seems so out of place to most of the artists. Building these things is like running downhill to us; we'll do it every time unless somebody stops us and turns us round. Down in my part of the country the same thing happened some years back, on the domestic scale. Money with us seems to just naturally bow down to wood and stone of a fairly monotonous design, a real icon. You'd be surprised—I hope you'll come south—to see the steps and the porticoes you'll meet at every turn along the rivers down there. Doric temples; Pæstum and Girgenti for family use. Slave labor of course."

"Still, you really had the forests, the living columns that are supposed to have furnished the suggestion for such building in the first place—though where the trees ever were in Greece—"

"Yes, but trees can suggest arches too. Left to ourselves, we never lay a Gothic brick."

"I've heard of your plantation dwellings," Silvain said. "They must be enormously picturesque, in that setting."

Steele considered this. "That's hardly the word, it seems to me. When things get turned around historically and start facing the other way, we are apt to call them picturesque, but they are much more in the line of fables than pictures. When the lion and the lizard take over, the photographer withdraws and the moralist steps up."

Silvain laughed. "Well, nobody has ever called me a moralist, and my friends, at least, don't call me a photographer, but I hope you'll ask me down in some capacity."

"I suppose you would think I had gone crazy if I were to tell you that I believe Nora has fallen in love with you."

The casual voice in which she managed to say it made it sound worse even than she thought it would; made it seem impossible that she should be saying it at all.

They had finished breakfast; she had timed her question so that no matter what the Senator answered —even if he didn't answer at all—they wouldn't have to sit there pretending to go on eating. He had already put his napkin down by his plate and picked his newspaper up and in another minute would be saying: "Well, Sabrina—" and getting up himself. She looked at him with a queer feeling in her chest. What was going to happen instead?

For a minute nothing did. He didn't do any of the things she had imagined him doing; not even laugh. She was beginning to wonder if he had understood—

"No, Sabrina, I shouldn't. I have such a high opinion of your sanity that no matter what you told me I should feel that I had to take it under serious consideration. All the same, there are some things I would rather you didn't tell me, unless you can give me some idea what to do about them."

Her chest felt better, but she waited for him to go on.

"This, for instance. Don't you see what a fix you would be putting me in? I couldn't even run away, as matters stand now, Congress in session and all; and if either of us suggested Mrs. Digby leaving, what could we say to Laura? You know how she feels about her friends."

"Of course I know." She could talk now. "That is where Nora has been so smart; she has positively be-witched Laura. There seems to be no end to the ways she has of working on her feelings—her imagination or whatever it is. And lots of times I don't believe it is good for her—"

He was looking at her seriously. "Go on," he said, and when she did not go on: "I am sure we both feel the same about a lot of things, Sabrina. We would be glad to see Laura more interested in all the various—interests, we have to call them, I suppose, even when they are not that to her. There are so few things she cares about, but for those she always cares a great deal."

"I know," she said. They both knew; they did not have to talk about Laura at all.

"And when you say that it is not good for her to listen to Mrs. Digby's yarns," he went on, "I am not sure that I quite agree with you. Laura doesn't read much, you know; this may be a substitute. Some of them are very pretty."

"I know they are; and getting prettier."

Now he was smiling. "We will just have to go slow, Sabrina. The human situation is always precarious. I often think it has no relation to actuality at all. It is just a sort of nebulous footbridge spanning most of the facts. We've got to walk delicately, like poor old Agag."

Going to his office he thought again of poor old Agag, who ought to be remembered occasionally for something besides the report that he came delicately to meet his doom. Surely the bitterness of death is past—he said that, so he must have come hopefully too. Hoping to escape death, or just not to mind it? The thing that made the Bible splendid was precisely this cloudiness. What a loss it would be if by means of revised versions or up-to-date revelations the light ever came through entirely. The result would be too dreadful to contemplate; it would be like taking away the atmosphere from the earth—robbing it of its earthly weather. Who wanted a scorched open place where everything was plain? It would be giving up more for truth than it could possibly be worth to anybody. Seeing things too clearly was a mistake; just as he told Sabrina.

The things that Sabrina had told him were, however, becoming too clear in spite of him. He had better stop considering the nature of truth, or of beauty either, and put in the rest of the time between where he was and the Capitol in meditating on whatever difference there was between them and love. For there was a difference, in spite of Plato.

Who was it that had the long-with-love-acquainted eyes? It would go for any man of an age to be long acquainted with anything, he supposed. *Splendidis longum valedico nugis*—and who said that? Somebody who had improved the acquaintance too assiduously, no doubt. But calling it splendid folly was no insurance against the damage it could do. Better recognize its potentialities at the outset and deal with it accordingly. And whatever was done in this case would have to be done by him. He would get no help from Nora. She would not help herself or let him help her; she insisted on being "lost."

"Listen to a dream I had: I was standing by a river, very wide, the way the rivers are in India when they are near the sea, and I was in terrible trouble because I had no way to get across. And then you came in a small boat and told me you would take me. You were dressed as the men dress out there, in a white dhoti, with a gold-embroidered cap on, and sandals on your feet, but I knew well that it was you and I got in. The moon was very bright on the water, and when we were in the middle of the stream I leaned over the side of the boat to catch with my hand the silver falling from the oar, and I saw there was a woman following the boat. She was below the water and could not speak, but with her hands she was entreating us to let her get into the boat, and I could see that it was I myself the woman was, and so I began to implore you to stop for her. 'O stop for me!' I said, and you laughed and told me I was dreaming. 'But it is no dream,' I said, and you still laughed and asked me how could I know that it was not a dream? So I began to think of all the ways I could prove it to you, and it seemed to me there would be none, and I began to cry terribly. And finally you told me there was one way. It was for me to jump from the side of the boat into the river, and then when you no longer saw me there before you, you could believe I had told you the truth about the woman. And that was what I did. The river was cold like death, but I only felt a great happiness, for now, I thought, he will believe me; but when I turned I saw that you were not watching what had happened. You were rowing on."

Where was it he first learned the wisdom of rowing on? No, not wisdom. That word was too august for any of his makeshift expedients. If he had a son to bring up—

Just what effect would it have on the behavior of young people if the language used in talking to them about it were rejuvenated too? The aphorisms in the copybook for instance—or did they have copybooks these days? Be good and you will be happy. Be good and you will be lonesome; somebody had tried that, but a child would miss the point. Be happy and you will be good.—The really helpful thing would be just to show him, less aphoristically, that what he should be was so interested in something all the time that he couldn't stop to think about whether he was good and happy or not. It might not be a bad idea, at some stage of a child's education, to try substituting the idea of art for the idea of morality. Revising the catechism might be too serious an experiment—God is an Artist and they who worship Him must do it by making things, forever and ever. That was what they did anyhow. Life must go on; people said that; but it wouldn't go on for them if they ever stopped making something else out of the something given to them.

It must have been back in the days when he was still consorting with Dr. Faustus, and other philosophers nearer his own age around the university, that he had begun experimenting with the æsthetic principle— his æsthetic principle—as a touchstone of conduct. Not with a view to salvation—heavens no! At that time he had never thought of himself as something he had to save; only to live with.

Entbehren sollst du, sollst entbehren—how did they put it in English?—

> *Thou shalt abstain—renounce—refrain!*
> *Such is the everlasting song*
> *That in the ears of all men rings.*

And why? Categorical imperative? Reward in heaven?—Why not because man is before anything else an artist, trying to get his life into a shape where he can bear the sight of it? *Entbehren sollst du*— Do without it, whatever it is, give it up, or you spoil the picture. Surely that is the reason we are always cutting off and adding on and making over, and even turning away altogether from what we call reality, like poor old Don Quixote, and riding away into something that looks prettier to us. And that is why telling a man that truth and beauty are the same thing, and that love is the same as either or both of the other two, is a pernicious deception. It's like teaching him that colors are synonymous, or sounds, and then expecting to like his painting or his music. Nothing is the same as anything. Nothing can be put in place of anything else. Love is so far from being truth or beauty that it has to be guarded incessantly to keep it either beautiful or true. Keeping love lovely is about the hardest job a man has to do. That, and making death acceptable—

It seemed to Steele, looking back, that the learned Doctor's experiences must have been a great help to him at that time; more than they had ever been to the Doctor. The spell of great poetry has a terrible strength in a language with which we are not familiar; the meaning comes to us in those unaccustomed words less as an impression than as a blow. The winter was chiefly memorable for this impact. It was not until the summer vacation offered him his one and only opportunity for European travel that he finally emerged from the cloudy splendors of the poetry and started out with scrip and staff to follow the poet. Geographically this time; he still remembered the pink and yellow map on which he had traced his *Wanderjhar*.

A third-class ticket and a pair of good legs had enabled him to more than fulfill his expectations in the matter of miles, but the spiritual fulfillments of the pilgrimage had been disappointing. Even the lack of money cannot keep a pilgrim from turning into a tourist when the way has been made too smooth before him. Led no longer by a dream but by tidy highways and liberal signboards, what could he expect to see when, for example, he climbed the Brocken, but the view? No whisper of the *Walpurgisnacht* remained for him, and he even doubted if much of it had been there for Goethe. And yet the time and the place and his disappointment had combined to give him something besides a rather inferior bit of mountain scenery: he could at least remember the Brocken as one of the places where he had begun to realize the intolerable nature of reality.

The winter began to surprise everybody in Washington by being very cold. Lafayette Square looked exactly like a Christmas card. The familiar evergreens became suddenly dark and mysterious under their white mantles, and the General was practically unrecognizable on a piebald horse, waving a hatful of snow. Nobody had thought about there being such a thing as sleighs in town until they surprisingly appeared, from the depths of old carriage-houses no doubt, and the muffled streets were gay with bells. It was festive; it was nordic. This last was a new word brought in with the new enthusiasm for Ibsen, whose plays were just then being presented at the New National Theater by a company from New York. Everybody was giving box parties and chafing-dish suppers and discussing heredity and suicide.

"How many of those people have killed themselves so far?" Steele asked after *Rosmersholm*. "I've only seen two plays, but they've netted me three suicides. What consciences they must have had then—or is it there?"

"Both, if you mean Ibsen's imagination, and that is certainly the only place where such people ever existed," the Honorable Cecil said. "The Puritans are a tax on your credulity, but at least they dealt with facts and not hallucinations."

"But they weren't, Cecil," Nora said. "They were the ghosts of facts that had already happened before the play begins, and to see their influence going on that way makes you realize more than anything else how fatal our actions are."

"And you must admit he gives you the feeling of having seen a lot of things you didn't see at all," Augustus Silvain said. "Your three suicides, Richard: all you had to go on this evening was what the housemaid presumably saw from the window. It must have been rather inevitable or we wouldn't have believed her as we did."

"And we hadn't seen the things that made it inevitable either," Sabrina said. "I do think it is wonderful that he can have conscience stalking around invisible that way. Shakespeare would have had the usual ghost, I suppose."

"An Elizabethan audience would have demanded it, don't you think so?" the Honorable Cecil said. "Included in the price of the ticket."

"And think what an Athenian audience demanded. The Furies were no bit part from all I can learn," Silvain said.

"How would it do to present a really economical

tragedy once in a while, with nobody's conscience in it, visible or invisible?" Steele said. "Something like the last scene in Revelation, where the accuser has been cast down and can't do any more accusing? Think how much extra action you could have in a play where nobody sat and brooded."

"But not having a conscience would be not having a memory, wouldn't it? Not having a past at all, really," Sabrina said.

"Well, let's don't have them, then. Time: morning of a new day. Dragging a past along is a clumsy thing to do, even in real life, and in a play it's boring. Imagine how refreshing not to have the maid and the butler telling you what has already happened! Just let everything begin right there before your eyes. Real creation, not the old cause-and-effect business."

"But then it wouldn't be in the least like reality, Richard," Laura said.

"Anyhow, it wouldn't hurt to try it on the stage, just to see how we would like it."

"The Man without a Past. Nice name for a play," Silvain said. "The country with no history. It is a sort of shadow—history; a blight on the future, in a way. We would be freer without any; too free."

"Imagine it!" Nora said. "The only thing that makes people behave even as well as they do is remembering what happened to them when they didn't. If I were you, Laura, I should be afraid to trust myself to a man who wanted to just chuck all his—mistakes, to speak politely—so he could turn right around and make the same ones over again."

Steele shook his head. "Couldn't do it. They couldn't be the same. That's the merit of the system: you'd never have but the one chance at anything. So you might want even your sins to do you credit. But while we are still on the old plan, Mrs. Digby, may I have the same cup of coffee over again? It was delicious."

The silver coffee-urn where Nora sat was brightly flushed on the side where the firelight touched it; the candles and the chafing-dish contributed their individual flames to the glow of the warm room. "A night like this—our weather plus Ibsen's—is nice to be in out of—if you like your prepositions that way; I always do." He took the cup she handed him, and noticed that the side of her face was rosy too. Her eyes—on any plan they could never be the same.

It seemed to Sabrina that nobody had the right to look the way Nora did sometimes. Just now she was

excited over the play. She was like something in a
song. All the same, she made you see what Ibsen had
in mind when he wrote those things. There was an
undercurrent of something dangerous below all that
sweetness and sparkle; dangerous to herself as much as
to anybody else. She was always talking about fate,
and being bound to the wheel of life; poetic, but not
very good for you, and especially not good for Laura,
whether it took the place of books or not. That kind
of books wouldn't be good for her either. According
to Laura, Nora really believed in suicide. It ran in her
family. They took that way out, as she expressed it,
when they had tied things into a knot for themselves
—and everybody else no doubt. Which was what Nora
was doing right now, it seemed to Sabrina—right
under Laura's eyes. The Senator's too, for that matter.
It would be impossible to convince him that a woman
could be in love with him to the point of making her
desperate—Sabrina too was excited over the play.

"There is one respect," Silvain said, "in which he
falls pretty far short of the other great dramatists, ad-
mitting that he is one: his characters never stand out
as types, the way Shakespeare's do, for instance. Those
Norwegian blondes of his never get out of the theater;

they are always some actress you have seen in the part; the latest, or the best, maybe. You can think of Portia or Juliet almost in the abstract, or Goethe's Gretchen. Perhaps he makes them that way on purpose; that may be what a playwright ought to do. It gives the actor a better chance at creation; instead of having to compete with what everybody in the audience brought along already created, he can make something of his own."

"I believe you are right," Steele said. "I have often thought that when people say, 'He didn't *act* Hamlet, he *was* Hamlet,' it may not be the compliment they mean it for. If there is any sense in it at all, it could only mean that Booth or Forbes-Robertson or whoever they are talking about stuck to the good old Hamlet type, which he certainly did not create and may not even prefer. But in that case, Silvain, you should not be allowed to paint a Juliet that everybody would recognize. As I see it, it is just another argument in favor of abolishing the past."

Laura had never had an engagement book before she came to Washington. At home nobody made engagements ahead. They were just invited and went

Nobody made calls or had days at home; they visited one another when they felt like it. But here, in what she called the worst of the season, she and Sabrina had to really keep their minds on calling, or staying where they could be called on, when the proper days rolled round. Almost all the days there were too, by the time they did the Cabinet and the Supreme Court and Congress and their own day—the Senate— and the Legations. And in all kinds of weather. That had seemed to her the biggest difference of all, until she got used to it. She still found herself saying, "Isn't it a pretty day?" to people who had evidently not noticed whether it was or not. In the country the weather was more important than almost anything else. She couldn't remember ever opening her eyes in the morning without looking out to see what kind of day it was, and always at night she or Richard or somebody would step out on the porch and say, "I believe it is going to clear off," or, "It looks like we're going to get our rain," or something else as cheerful as possible, to go to bed by. Not mentioning the weather seemed a loss somehow. It was like not noticing the moon.

Sabrina still mentioned the weather, but she enjoyed living in town. Laura could see that. She was not especially sociable in the sense of liking to talk, but she never got tired of watching people and making up her mind about them—unless she had made it up already. And she approved of parties not only as a pleasure but as a duty too.

"I think it is right for people to dress up for each other and get out the best china and have nice things to eat. It means something; it isn't just an empty show. Even savages do it in some form or other."

"But you never really get to know anybody this way, Sabrina, while they are all trying to be just alike."

"But they can't be. That makes it so interesting. There's as much difference this way as any other; more, really. It's when you get to know people well that you find out how much alike they all are. Anyhow, I'd rather compare them on their good behavior. I know you like to be taken into the family, but I would much rather be company."

They had made two Cabinet calls and were driving home through the wintry streets, which at this hour were full of movement; everybody driving home to get dressed and go somewhere else. Sabrina loved to watch the reflection of so many carriage lamps in the wet pavement. O them golden streets!—She thought o the long dark roads at home, the ground soft and splashy under the horses' feet. She had enjoyed her two teas immensely, and had met some delightful people at one of them: new people, from—she had forgotten where they said their home was. But they hadn't talked about it, or about Washington either; they had talked about Peter Ibbetson, and from there they had somehow begun saying nonsense rhymes to each other. The man—Mr. Huntington—had a wonderful collection; she had tried to remember some of them to tell the Senator, but of course she couldn't. She hadn't held on to even that much about them, and yet she felt she knew them better than if they had told her how old their children were, and asked her about the schools in Washington. It must be wrong for her to feel that way; it was not being interested in humanity.

In Laura's sitting-room it was too dark to do anything without a lamp and too early to light one. The curtains had not been drawn, but there was little pretense of light in the wintry sky outside. Even Coq d'Or, though he had not retired, seemed at a loss for anything else to do. Hopping aimlessly from perch to swing, he made for once no sound.

Steele had let himself in with his latchkey and come directly upstairs. Through the open door he could see Laura's rocker drawn up in front of the grate, where a low fire was burning. He came behind it as he always did, as she always expected him to do, and was leaning down to lay his tributary kiss on the dark crown of her hair, when he saw all at once that it was not Laura's crown, but Nora's. She had to all appearances not heard him come in; she sat so still he thought she must certainly be asleep; but when he moved around where he could see her face, he was sure she had not been.

"What has happened?" she said, looking up at him with actual terror in her eyes. "Why are you here alone? Oh my dear, my dear, what has happened?"

She reached both her hands up to him, then put them suddenly before her face and began to sob with all the abandonment of a child.

He sat down in the chair beside her and waited for her to stop. "Were you asleep, Nora?" he asked gently. "Did I startle you?"

She shook her head.

"Has Laura gone out?—Sabrina?"

She nodded.

"Will you take your hands down so I can look at you, Nora? Now tell me what all this is about."

She had obediently removed her hands, but it was still some time before she could control her voice, and then it was only to tell him that she did not know—that she had heard nothing, seen nothing. "I only knew that something had happened—something very bad—oh, sad, sad! I knew my heart was breaking because you were here alone."

"But I am not," he said, smiling at her. "Aren't you here with me? Weren't you already here? You were alone yourself before I came in—for how long, by the way? And where did Laura go? Did Jessie tell you?"

The maid did not know where they had gone, Nora told him. "She said she had been expecting them back for some time, so I came up here to wait.—Listen! There they are!" She jumped up. She was smiling.

Somehow she always managed to be gay. This time he could not find it in his heart to doubt the reality of the terror that had possessed her, however unreal its occasion, and he was amazed at the swiftness with which she threw it off. Or had it vanished of itself in the relief of hearing Laura's voice in the hall and knowing her fears, whatever they were, unfounded?

He was sure, though she had not said so, that they had something to do with Laura. Sitting there in front of the fire, waiting, listening, she must have fallen into one of the curious psychological states that were her specialty—and a highly inconvenient one at that, he thought. A faculty whose findings were so little to be relied on seemed to him of doubtful benefit to its possessor, and a positive nuisance to those who might fancy themselves implicated in its dim forebodings. Though, on the other hand, having it more trustworthy, or even more explicit, might make it still less desirable to have around.

There was company for dinner that evening, and then he had some writing to do. It was late before Steele had time to think very much about the afternoon's experience. Not that thinking could help in a case like this— Like this? What other case ever was like this—this whole business of Nora? The mind had an incorrigible tendency to generalize. At the university they had taught him—or thought they had— a lot about Occam's Razor; this might be a good place to use it. Or perhaps, since it was a place where a man had neither precedent nor memory to guide him, it would be better for him not to try to think his wa

out of it at all; just live it out; a little like that char-
acter with no past they had been discussing awhile
back.

And yet how disappointing, how shocking really,
it must be for Sabrina to see him handling the situation in this way, after all she had done to save it! He
wondered how long she had waited to tell him what
she did—to screw her courage to the sticking-place.
He had been touched to see the way the pretty color
left her face as she was speaking—left all her freckles
showing. To her the issue was as plain as if she had
told him the house was on fire. She knew what any
man would do: put out the fire or else get out himself
—saving his wife first, naturally. What must she think
of him, letting the weeks go by without doing anything? She would feel that she must explain the nature of fire to him next. It would never occur to her
that he might be warming his hands at the blaze.

On the other side of Lafayette Square the White
House stood softly illuminated among the trees; not
for a reception, but a musicale. Laura didn't mind a
small party, even at the White House, and she loved
music. She still played the piano sometimes, on sum-

mer evenings at the plantation, but she hardly ever sang any more. She and Richard used to sing duets. The parlor at home was a wonderful room to sing in, the ceilings were so high. *Don Giovanni, Trovatore*— they had even done things like that. *"Ah che la morte'* — Richard's voice was really lovely; even in speaking it was; and to think how long it had been since she had heard him sing! Only whistle, when he was dressing or sometimes when he was just thinking.

The Blue Room was nice for music too; so *intime* Irène would say. That was her favorite word when she talked about what went on in Washington. No other capital in the world had such a friendly atmosphere, she was always saying. Imagine being asked to dinner by the President, or just dropping in to call as you would on one of your neighbors— Irène could not get used to it. And Mr. Silvain too— "This cozy little town," he called it. Richard had asked him to visit them this summer at the plantation. Laura wondered what he would think of that. Irène still thought the South must be like Russia. Which one of the other countries would he think it was like? The poor South! It always had to be like something else before people would think of it as anything at all. He had asked her

f she would let him make some sketches of her, for a
portrait maybe. Not here in Washington, of course;
n the country, where they would have more time, he
aid. As if she were not ten times busier there than she
ould ever be anywhere else!

"How do you like her, Mrs. Steele?" The young
inger by the piano was bowing her thanks to the gen-
ral approval. Silvain, who had heard her in Paris,
as particularly enthusiastic. "They called her the
erfect Mélisande over there—in their ignorant
rench way; they haven't heard your husband's ideas
n the subject of those abstractions. She used to oblige
iem by looking the part even on the rue de la Paix.
's her own hair too, those braids."

Laura thought she was lovely. "But I didn't under-
and the French very well. What was it she said about
ie water?"

"Oh, she—tell her the story, Richard; I don't want
spoil it by putting it wrong end first." He remem-
red there was something in Laura's own story that
e must be careful to go around. That accounted for a
t of things in her, no doubt. The stillest face he had
er seen. Nice lines. But paint would not be the
ing he wanted; those sketches, if he ever made them,

143

ought to be developed in another medium. "Look, I believe she is going to give us an encore," he said.

Walking home across the Square, Silvain was talking again about the coziness of Washington. "And it has in addition all the *sic transit* charm of something that is on its way out—on the brink of a tremendous change. We can be perfectly sure that if we woke up, say fifty years from now, we wouldn't find any of this to speak of. Which would be sad, but probably not so sad as what we would find in its place. I imagine the only thing we would recognize would be each other."

"Hardly that, I should say, if you really mean fifty years," Steele said.

"Make it five hundred and I would still mean it. Not we three individuals, but whatever was walking here instead of us would be perfectly recognizable. We could talk to them right this minute if we met them, and understand each other perfectly—after a few little preliminaries of a mechanical nature, such as airships and motor-vehicles, had been disposed of."

"In that case I imagine they would not be walking; they'd be riding in the preliminaries," Steele said. "All the same, I see your drift. I've often wondered myself why we lag so far behind our own inventions."

looks every now and then as if they might be running away with us, but we always find ourselves pretty much where we were; back with the old landmarks, the rooted sorrows and the prehistoric joys. This night might be considered one of the joys, after the winter we've been having. Like spring, isn't it, Laura? Time to start plowing."

They walked slowly through the Square, toward their own lighted windows on the other side; past the General in his open space where the moon shone down, and Laura's bench in the stenciled shadow of the still leafless trees. She had stopped listening to the conversation. She was wondering if anybody had remembered to plant the sweet peas. Last year they had planted them too late and just about half as deep as they ought to have been.

The Digbys were leaving Washington before anybody else did this year; they were even going to miss the spring. "And maybe not be back before Christmas," Nora said dejectedly. "Count the months, Laura, and see how much older we shall all be! And it is in England, of all places, that I shall be spending them—a beastly hole at any season, in my opinion."

"But not in spring, Nora! The English springtime is so famous—"

"I know: Now that April's there. I have seen Aprils in England when I did not see the sun—not enough to notice, at any rate. It was a poet said that, and he was not in England when he said it, either."

"Do you ever go to Ireland, Nora?"

"Never. I have been there twice in my whole life, the first time when I was too little to remember, and the last time it was to fight with the lawyers over my mother's estate; and Irish lawyers, I can assure you, Laura, are the worst on earth. Still," she said, smiling suddenly, "there were some funny things that happened in that famous case. My uncle—my grandfather's illegitimate son he was—you would never believe there would be a scoundrel like that in any family, and so of course it must be in mine that he was. Some day I will tell you that wild tale."

"But if it hadn't been for that—for the lawsuit—would Ireland have seemed nice to you, do you suppose?"

Nora shook her head. "Perhaps one always quarrels with the world when one has seen too much of it. Many times I envy you the little you have seen."

"Maybe you would have been happy to stay in India," Laura said.

"Perhaps, for then I knew nothing of any other place. There was a prince out there, a Rai, who wanted my father to give me to him. When I was very young that was; I believe I could not have been more than fourteen years old when he asked to marry me, and promised my father all the things he would do for me. Build me a house was one of them, so that I need not live with any other women."

"But surely your father—"

"No. But I think very likely I would have done that too. Then imagine all the lands that would have been between us, Laura, all the mountains and the seas! We are just in the hands of fate. We do not know what we want, nor even what it is many times when we have it. Shall I tell you a story about one of the great Sufi teachers? They are Mohammedans, and though you would perhaps not see their difference from other Indians, to them it is vast. You would never believe how deeply they distrust one another, how—"

"Tell me the story, Nora."

"Their legends are different too, of course, and some of them are beautiful," Nora went on, "so listen about this man. He was not only wise and good but also very rich, and when he heard a great deal about a woman in another province who was said to be the loveliest in India, he determined to have her for his wife. So he arranged with her parents that he would build for her a palace—a little as Faiz Rai would have done for me—and when it was finished she was to come, all veiled of course, and then he would see her for the first time. But when at last the moment came and the veil was lifted from her face, instead of the bride he had been dreaming of, it was the angel Azrael —do you know that angel, Laura, which one it is, I mean?"

"Isn't it death?" Laura said.

Nora nodded. "It was the angel Azrael who stood before him. Then he was terrified and fell on his knees and cried to the angel: 'Have mercy!' and the angel's answer was: 'I am Mercy.' Isn't it a lovely story, Laura? Many times when life seems bad and bitter to me, I remember it. It seems a little bad and bitter to me now, because I do not want to go away."

Everybody knew she did not want to go away. Everybody lamented with her that she should have to miss the Washington spring, the parties on the lawns the tulips in the parks. Nobody sympathized with the Honorable Cecil even when his sceptered isle was called a beastly hole right to his face. Nor did he ask for sympathy; as usual he smiled.

In Congress it was the currency question. The desk in Steele's office was piled with the outpourings of his constituents, who had all turned out to be experts on the subject, he said. Even the ones who had never learned to spell could still express themselves with fluency on the relative merits of gold and silver—the two sides of the shield on which it seemed to him his party was likely to be carried from the field.

"A lady to see you, sir."

He looked up and was surprised to see that it was Nora. One of the things he had told her she must not do—

"I know," she said. "I told the doorman I had an appointment. He thought I looked harmless."

"Not like an army with banners?" He placed a chair for her, glancing at the clock.

"I am not going to keep you," she said. "Sit down where you were, at your desk. I had to come. I never have a chance to talk to you. There are always people."

"There should be people, Nora. Our lives have been arranged that way."

"I know," she said. "Long ago, without a thought for each other. It is a thing I shall never understand: that I should not have known from the beginning that you would come. Even when I was a child, in India, that I should not have seen you like an angel in the sky—or a cloud that would put out the sun! And now I wonder if you know what it is I want to say."

He shook his head. "I am only afraid it means trouble, Nora; trouble for somebody. Wouldn't it be better not to say it?"

"No," she said, "because I am going away. It is something for you to think about while I am gone. It is something about you, who are always so strong; like a ship that goes before the wind, so that you have not only your own strength but the wind's strength too. What hope can there be for me who am going the other way? I am beaten to pieces by the waves that carry you along. Will you remember that?"

He looked at her in silence. Where had he heard these things, or read them, or dreamed them? Surely women did not say them sitting in an office, across a table littered with the currency question?

"If you would only turn to me a little," she said, "here in the trough of the sea. If you would be only a little less strong, less sure, so that I could think of you sometimes as I do of other men. I have known so many in my life, though I am not old, and not of one of them have I ever been afraid."

"Afraid, Nora? What are you saying?—"

"Of what you can do to me; of what you can make me suffer through this strength of yours. What is it in the Bible?—The winds and the sea obey him. That was God, of course, but what is the difference, if you are always on that side?" Her eyes, which had not left his face, were suddenly deep in tears.

"Come now!" he said. "Have you forgotten that you told me when we talked of this the first time, that you didn't care much for the people who were always on that side—saints and things? Why are you trying to make me into one of them?" She would not smile. "My dear Nora, can't you see that it is better not to talk about these things? Unless we are prepared to be poets—which is maybe what you are. It would be better not even to think of them—"

"It is for that very reason that I have come here now," she said. "Because I know you will not think of them any more when I have gone. That too you are able to do—to put me out of your thoughts as you would a dream when you wake up in the morning. Not once will you say to yourself: 'I have taken this woman's soul and put it in my own breast, and so what can she do without it?'"

In utter helplessness he looked away—at anything; at the papers on his desk, at the clock—

As usual, she came to her own aid. "I promised not to stay," she said, getting up; the tears were gone, her eyes—it was better not to see what happened there. The thing they promised him was not to be found on earth; that he knew.

"Since I, my lord, am nothing unto thee," she said— "Listen, in Hindustani it is this—"

III · The Statue

SUNDAY EVENING at the plantation was always longer than other evenings for the reason that supper was so late. Mattie went to church in the afternoon and didn't get back to cook it until after dark. It was hotter too, for some other reason; probably because nobody had anything special to do—at least nobody but Richard, who always had people coming, or had to go somewhere. Everybody else took naps, and then got dressed and sat around and talked. Laura thought Sunday might be a little like Russia after all. It was not her favorite day though, not by any means. She was always a little glad when it was over. This was the third one since Mr. Silvain had been there, and it would soon be over. Mattie was singing in the kitchen, one of the mournful hymns she always brought back from church, and Jake had begun to set the table; he was rattling the silver worse than usual, it seemed to her, when she came downstairs in her white dress and went into the parlor, where Richard and Mr. Silvain were still talking by the window, with nothing but the darkness outside and no lamp.

"Oh, you poor benighted things," she said. "Do let's have a little light on the subject—"

On the plantation having a light did not mean pressing a button or even just striking a match. It meant going for a lamp, and hoping it had been duly filled, the wick trimmed, the chimney cleaned, and the shade adjusted. She came back presently, holding one in both hands, the light thrown upward on her face.

"There is something very pretty in Greek about ladies holding lamps," Silvain said.

"But ladies don't know Greek," she said; "except Sabrina of course, and that was just an accident—because she had that kind of a father." She set the lamp down in the center of the table and turned toward the two men who stood watching her, her face now lighted by a smile.

"Well, there's something pretty in English too—American, rather—

Helen, thy beauty is to me—

What is the part about the 'lighted window niche,' Richard?"

"Let's see," Richard said, going over to the bookcase.

"Not now, Richard: supper. Mattie has hot rolls, and you know she doesn't like for them to stand a minute. Did Sabrina go upstairs?"

"But in spite of 'the glory that was Greece'"—Silvain, now buttering his roll, had his mind still on the poem—"it occurs to me your Edgar Allan Poe might supply that American-Gothic imagination you were talking about, Richard: 'Ramparts plumed and pallid,' for example. What do you think about it, Miss Sabrina? I believe his Greek is a good deal more accidental than yours is: his 'pyrogene' and the rest."

"I told him about your father: how you happened to study it," Laura explained.

"We always apologize for you, Sabrina," Richard said.

"You needn't—anything that little. Where did Poe come into your life, Mr. Silvain? Since you came over here?" Sabrina asked him.

"In England. We have him in French, of course; awful; and in German. He's a little like Bürger, isn't he, Richard? *Die Todten reiten schnell*—that means 'The dead ride swiftly,' Mrs. Steele. Both these poets had a great deal to say about phantoms." Silvain was no longer afraid of making such mortal references in Laura's presence.

In the weeks since he came, his artist's penetration had made him familiar with many things about her besides her stillness and her "lines." The sketches suggested in Washington had hardly progressed at all down here, and he had learned by this time that they never would, unless he made up his mind to draw her peeling something or shelling something, which was not in line with his idea. The end of these activities seemed ever more distant and his departure was drawing near. Conversationally, however, they had advanced. They had taken walks in the late afternoon, and Jake had taken them in the barouche to see whatever there was in the neighborhood that she thought might interest an artist—unless Sabrina had already showed it to him when they went horseback riding. In this way they had walked down to the pond on more than one occasion and had driven over to the little cemetery near the church to put flowers on Rickie's grave. He had only a little headstone now,

with his name and dates, but some time they were going to have a monument—a statue, Laura said.

Silvain looked about him at all the angels and the
scrolls. In a near-by lot there was a lamb: an ancient
lamb, much mildewed.

"Just what did you have in mind, Mrs. Steele?" he
asked her. "Or had you got that far?"

She told him they were waiting for Richard to have
more time. "He thinks I ought to go to Europe first
and see some of the most beautiful ones over there. I
have never been, you know."

"I know. It's something for you to look forward to,
isn't it—for both of you?"

She did not answer. They were sitting on a little
white bench under the shade of a maple tree, where
she could look at the floral arrangement she had just
completed, and she now went over to make some improvement in it, her white skirts spreading around her
on the grass. "I expect we had better go back," she
said when she stood up, glancing at the sun. "Jake has
to milk, you know."

"Does it seem strange to you," she asked him as they
were driving home, "that I never do look forward to
things—not even to going to Europe? If you had to

stay in a place like this, where nothing happens—nothing important to anybody else, I mean—it would ruin your life, I expect. Maybe you couldn't go on being an artist, even, in such a place. Everything has to come from something else, doesn't it?"

He looked at her, trying to guess her meaning. "Unless one is terribly strong internally; in one's own nature—" he ventured.

"Or terribly weak? Isn't it considered a sort of weakness to be satisfied, as far as the future is concerned? To be always looking back into the past for what you want?"

"It is considered very unusual at any rate—especially in anyone as young as you. You let Richard bring you to Europe, whether you want to come or not. The sooner you get that into your past, the better. I do agree with you that looking back is lots of fun, though I enjoy looking forward too. I even enjoy some things while they are still happening. My visit here for instance. You have all been endlessly good to me. I haven't even minded the heat the rest of you talk about so much."

His artist's penetration could hardly have led him to suspect that this conversation, driving with Laura

along the country road, would turn out to be one of
the things he would look back on very often. Not because it was fun, but because of the associations that
gathered round it. For one thing, it was the last serious
talk they ever had together, and this made him realize, when the time for reckoning came, how many of
such talks they must have had. He was destined to feel
that in those few weeks he had learned to know her
very well indeed.

It was on the whole a nice summer. If they had
talked about the heat, that was because they always
did, whether they had any right to complain or not.
Sabrina had a new horse and a new admirer. Not Mr.
Silvain; he was gone now, anyway; this was a boy she
had known all the time, but the admiration was new.
He had been off to college; getting his eyes opened,
the Senator said. In the matter of girls, at least. "It
seems to me he still squints a little in regard to some
other things though; less important matters; philosophy for instance. How does it seem to you?"

"Don't I too? Why ask me?"

"Two squints might bring it into focus. Anyhow, I
would like to know what you think of what he thinks

of those books he's been bringing you. I had never even heard of Nietzsche when I was Henry's age."

"I've never heard of him now except from Henry. He seems to be a 'trend.'"

"That's why we want to keep our eye on him. If life or literature either is 'trending' in that direction, I want to know about it in time."

"In time for what?"

"To take steps, as we say in the legal profession. We can't just sit still and do nothing."

"Because it sounds undemocratic?"

"It doesn't sound aristocratic either—not to me. That's what he calls it, I know: Aristocratic Radicalism is what Henry is letting us in for, I believe; but his perfected individual, his Superman, strikes me as being a pretty uncouth specimen: on the order of Genghis Khan, I should say, or Attila. Ask him about it and let me know what he says."

"He told me he wanted to ask you about Goethe. He says nobody feels that way—the way you feel—about him any more. I had told him."

"Well, we all have our ups and downs. But I'll be glad to take Henry on for a debate whenever he feels like it. There's my horse."

From where she sat at the breakfast table Sabrina watched through the open window while he rode away under the trees that were already rolling their shadows up and getting ready for the day's conflagration. She wondered if riding along the dusty road was as good for thinking as walking to the Capitol. What did he think about anyway?—besides politics, of course. Not about any of the things he said to her; he just said them without thinking, just to amuse her. Did he ever think about Nora? Nora had written to him, once anyhow. He had taken the letter when Jake brought the mail, and put it in his pocket before he looked at the rest. Her letters were lovely; Laura read the ones to her out loud. They were so funny; Nora had a wonderful sense of humor.

It must be a queer experience for a man to be in love with one woman, the way the Senator was with Laura, and have another woman feeling about him the way Nora did. How much of it ever got put into words? What would she say in a letter, for instance?— Sappho to Phaon. That Greek of hers kept bobbing up. Intelligent as Nora was, she ought to realize how hopeless it would be—trying to make the Senator feel anything but a friendly interest in any woman except

Laura. She had probably never met with a perfect love before, in any land where she had ever been, and so she simply didn't understand it enough to see how she was wasting her time. And Laura, on the other hand, just took it for granted. It was the only kind of love she understood at all.

Sabrina got her hat and her garden scissors and went out to cut the flowers, such as they were. Larkspur and petunias mostly; the roses were gone. There would be more in the fall, of course, but then they wouldn't be here to see them. She stood at the top of the steps and looked off across the lawn where a few yellow leaves from the elm trees were already lying on the grass. She stood quite still, trying to see the place deserted as it would be then, to hear the approaching silence. The country was always sad, if you stopped to think about it. Country homes: people talked about them as if they were sweet and cozy, like a nest. They were something to break your heart over, every one of them; not only the abandoned ones or the ones that had burned down, but even when people went on living in them. When she thought about the tears of things, it was always country things, but whether it was the ones that were always changing or the ones that stood still and saw them change, she could not decide.

When she and Mr. Silvain went riding together, he was surprised to see how often they would pass a place where the house had burned down; only the tall brick chimneys left standing. In Europe, she supposed, they would not have been frame houses, or not big ones, the way these were. He said it gave him the strangest feeling every time they came across one of those chimneys standing among the trees. "It's the most meaningless vestige I ever saw anywhere. Not like anything left over from life at all. Of course to you it has associations; you know what it stands for: so many fireplaces, so many floors; you can figure out how big the house must have been. To me it doesn't even suggest a human habitation."

"Isn't that because there is nothing left to go with it? Not even the ashes of anything."

"There is as much as some towers have. More than an altar, or a well. Think of what they mean! And the thing stands there so horribly intact: as if it refused to be artistic, or historical, or to blend with the landscape even. That's the beauty of a ruin, you see: nature opens her arms to it." Mr. Silvain was very interesting. She knew she would see a lot of things in a different light, now that she had seen them a little through his eyes. But even if he didn't think the chimneys looked sad, they were.

Henry was a tall young man with nice eyes. This last year had improved him so much that Sabrina thought he might turn out to be good-looking in the end. It occurred to her too that he must have been doing a lot of thinking, all this time he had seemed to be doing nothing—just being lanky and cheerful. One year at the University of Virginia couldn't possibly have put all those ideas into anybody's mind. Minerva wasn't going to spring full-panoplied out of Henry's head. Even the Senator seemed to think his ideas were worth listening to. That surprised her more than anything. But it didn't seem to surprise Henry in the least.

"You understand, sir, that I don't consider myself in a position to criticize his poetry. I am going to study German next year, but I doubt if I get around to Goethe. It's the man himself that seems to me to fall so far short of the human maximum he's been set up

to be. He was pedantic—you'll admit that—and pro-
vincial. It seems to me he was just about the opposite
of the type you would admire."

"That's nice of you, Henry. I don't admire either of
those qualities, even when we find them in a great
man. I don't admire them in Dr. Johnson either.
Stodgy. The ideal of normality is apt to be stodgy, I'm
afraid; but every now and then, every few hundred
years or so, we are supposed to have a normal genius,
paradoxical as it sounds. Your friend Nietzsche, I
gather, is a long way off the norm. I've been looking
over some of those books you left here."

They were sitting on the porch, with no moon to
light their faces, but Sabrina could see Henry's sil-
houette against the bright window behind him become suddenly alert. "The trend," she thought.

"But isn't it true, sir, that the really great thinkers—
the great teachers, I mean—have always been abnormal? Take Socrates. Take Jesus—"

"But we have just taken Nietzsche. I want to know
how you really feel about the program he outlines for
the human race. I take it the men are all to be—
heroes, let us say; and the women—?"

"Well, of course he believes the whole social fabric
has got to be changed; rewoven, I suppose you might
say."

"Good. Rewoven. That's a good figure; helps us to
see it as a tapestry, doesn't it? All the bright figures
of the past—

> *Hector and Ajax will be there again,*
> *Helen will stand upon the wall to see—*

Do they still read Matthew Arnold?—Nietzsche,
from what I gather, isn't going to let Helen even be a
spectator in the game—or am I mistaken?"

"Well, you see, sir—"

"I know. A lot of those great teachers had the same
idea; but they never seemed to get very far with it
for some reason. Women, or woman, as they call her,
made their biggest problem. They would no more
than get her down where they wanted her in the
human scale than she would decide to just stop being
human altogether and become a goddess, or a Virgin,
or something else unmanageable like that: an idea, or
a Force. It would be a lot simpler to always put her
where she wants to go, wherever it is, right in the beginning. You'll agree with me, won't you, Sabrina?"

"Don't I always?"

"Well, that being the case, I'll leave Nietzsche in your hands to speak my mind about. I've got something a whole lot less interesting to do. Know very much about bimetallism, Henry?—I hoped not."

Sabrina was always sorry when the Senator went in and left her with the current admirer, the current beau. Whoever he was, it was sure to be a come-down after the conversation they had been having, whatever that was. On this occasion Henry seemed to be thinking about something. She supposed it was still Nietzsche, but it turned out to be something else.

The summer was closing in. Laura, who had been saying "only another month" was beginning to count the weeks now. She always did that. Then she would start ticking off the days. It was enough to make anybody feel melancholy; even anybody who didn't mind going. "Do you suppose Nora will really not be back before Christmas?" Sabrina asked her. "You'll hate to not find her there. Did she say anything about it in her letter?"

"She didn't know yet; she said Cecil made a dark secret of it." Laura smiled. "She did say she was homesick, though. I'll read you the letter, this evening when Richard is here."

Sabrina looked at her. She was sewing, these days. Another of the season's changes. It meant the vegetables and the fruits were over. Rows and rows of jars. The squirrel's granary is full. That was the way Laura worked: instinctively, like a squirrel. She could think of anything while she did it, and did it so swiftly too.

Just now she was thinking of her letter. What did Nora mean by saying those things? Talking about sitting on doorsteps, as if nobody wanted to let her in? Did she think people were forgetting her? Didn't they write to her as much as she thought they should?—

"In London there is the Russian Ballet, and these pokey English have gone mad. I wish you could see the young Pavlova dance. It is one of the prettiest things in life altogether, besides being great art. She at least remembers the time when she had wings. Most of us have forgotten about that time. I read a story once about a woman who had been a swan and who one day found her long swan's feathers again, where her husband had hidden them, in his great fear of losing her. So what did she do?—I will tell you when I come home, and in the meantime I shall tell it to Pavlova, to make into a ballet. Did you hear me say 'come home'?—quite without thinking; but I will let it stand, now that I have thought. When one has no home, one should be permitted to sit by whatever hearth one chooses, or on whatever doorstep—"

"It only means that Nora lisps in numbers," Richard said, when she read the letter aloud in the evening after dinner. "For all we know, she may be a direct descendant of the Irish bards. Let's ask her some time."

She folded the letter and put it back in the envelope. Lying in her lap it was soon submerged under the rising tide of ruffles.

"I wonder if you remember, Richard," she said, after a long silence in the course of which Sabrina had said good-night and gone to bed, "a poem you read me once out of a magazine, that had this line in it—

I have forgotten you, long, long ago—

I don't remember the rest of it, or even who it was that wrote it, but I think it was supposed to be a man who had died, speaking to someone he had loved on earth."

He put down the pamphlet he was reading and gave her his full attention. He could not recall the poem, he told her. "Was there something in the letter that reminded you of it?"

"Everything reminds me of it," she said. "This summer, I mean. I keep thinking about how Rickie must be forgetting all the things here he used to know about. I don't know why that poem is so much sadder than it would have been if somebody else had said it *about* the person who had died—'He has forgotten you, long, long ago'— It seems to put him so far away, somehow, to say it about himself."

"I believe I see what you mean, Laura," he said after thinking a little. "This way it sounds less like forgetting than like another state of consciousness altogether. Poets do those things to us, darling. There is a catch in it, a trick of rhetoric. It can be beautiful and painful too sometimes, until we stop and think about it. You must remember, Laura, that people do not have to die in order to forget things. Living may be even a better way, for most of them. It seems to me sometimes that is what living really is—forgetting. I is the only way to have anything new. And think how painlessly we do it! We even imagine we are doing it on purpose most of the time.

"It is a good deal the same with loss," he said, after waiting for her to speak. "There are so many ways of losing things, and most of them we do not mind at all. A lot of them we call 'improvements.' It is the sudden changes we find so hard to bear. But do you know, Laura, I am beginning to think there is a trick there too: something that has to do with time. Time is a great mystery. Somebody has got to work on it. But not tonight, darling. Let's go out on the porch and walk up and down awhile, to make you sleepy. You are such a quiet girl, to do as little sleeping as you do these days. Why aren't you nervous and fussy, the way you have a right to be? You neglect your privileges. Better get something to put around you; it's actually cool out there." The summer was closing in.

In the circle of light made by the green-shaded lamp on his library table, Steele was writing to Sabrina. What could he say that would not make her sad? *Son of man, behold I take from thee the desire of thine eyes at a stroke, yet shalt thou neither mourn nor weep, neither shall thy tears run down.* Sabrina, in that empty house, must be written to with cheerfulness.

She would be standing on the porch when Jake came from the post office and handed her the letter. She would probably sit down on the steps and read it. Pretty weather, he hoped. In the country that always helped. Her Aunt Carrie would help too. Thank goodness she was a cheerful aunt. It really seemed as if nothing in life counted for more than cheerfulness. Life being what it was. And death—

How was it possible to be ever unprepared? And this time, looking back, he could see so many things that should have instructed him. The shadow had been waiting at every turn—the tireless referee. He had been willfully blind. And even now, how much was he willing to see? The mind was reluctant to do what was required of it—to see something familiar, something accepted as harmless, changed suddenly into a mortal agency. Laura had always had those intervals of sleeplessness; the tempo of her life had seemed in some way adjusted to them, and to doing without the so-called remedies continually offered her by sympathetic friends. "Only if a doctor gives it to you, Laura, and then always a little less, never a little more"—he must have told her that a hundred times, and this time, so far as they could learn, it was a prescription she had used before. He would never know as much about it as he would if he had been there. It had taken him all night and a part of the next day to get to her, even after they got the message to him. The trains in that section were bad. He had jumped on anything that was moving. It had been a nightmare journey; all the way she was flying before him; he had despaired of overtaking her. And then, when he did—how still! Long and still and white— "I never realized she was so tall." One always heard that. Not about anyone asleep. Only this—this more vital thing. *O nobly born, the time has come for thee to enter the path*— Was it a gesture of recognition?

And now, in this empty house, he must be cheerful. "It is open just a crack," he wrote; "enough to let me out and in and to present a front not too forbidding if anyone should come, but not enough I hope to let your imagination run around in it too much. I believe I will let you into the kitchen, though, for I know you will be surprised to see how many things Emma has remembered. I will even let you taste the coffee—though of course you know already by the smell—

"Walking to my office this morning I thought of the day that was beginning down there for you, an hour after the one here, as we choose to reckon it—my nine, by the clock on the post-office tower as I passed, your eight by the one in the hall. 'In the garden already,' I said to myself—'unless it is raining.' There I was, you see. I had you fixed in time and space, but not in weather. And that made me happier somehow; I hated to think there was nothing but a mathematical calculation between *here* and *there,* with me feeling about them as I did. All the same, I hoped it wasn't raining. We mustn't let it rain—not yet awhile. We must try to keep the weather golden, and try to think of nature as kinder than she is. Now if ever is the time to let her take out her tubes and brushes and color everything she will: the sunset, the past, the truth—"

And if she refuses? What if nature should decide that now was the time to teach him her real attitude toward life, to come at him with her teeth bared—no purpose, no pity, an insanity of force, destroying what she had labored longest to perfect? *Omega, thou art lord*— And after that? The mind was incorrigible: "And then what happened?" That is the end, my child. "And what comes after the end?" The beginning, naturally; of something else. Of knowledge? If God saw that we had nothing left, no toys, would He whisper the secret in our ear?

Sabrina's Aunt Carrie had come out in the garden, where she was cutting the last of the dahlias, to say she thought it would be a good idea to pick the last of the butter-beans. "I believe we are going to have a killing frost," she said. The garden was full of sunshine but the wind had changed. It was December; last things were happening fast.

"Maybe it would," Sabrina said. "You go ahead and start; I'll take the flowers in first. Don't you want your coat?" Her voice got louder and louder, for Aunt Carrie had already gone ahead and was halfway to the vegetable garden, her black and white gingham skirt blowing in the wind. She shouted back that a coat would "hamper" her.

Sabrina laughed, gathering up her heavy-headed flowers. One of the funniest things about living in the country was these long-distance conversations everybody carried on, hurrying in opposite directions, sending their voices back. There must be something in open spaces that made people want to shout.

"My, but you do pick fast!" she said, when she had got her own coat and her own basket and started down on her own side of the tall beanpoles. "And there seem to be quite a lot of them, taking the ones that aren't filled out yet."

"We'll have to leave the top ones for Jake; he has a longer reach," Aunt Carrie said. "I think they are nicer than ever at this time of year—these little green ones. Did you all make any tomato ketchup this summer? I always love it on butter-beans."

"I—I think so," Sabrina said. She didn't know what was in all those jars. The squirrel's granary— Oh, how could it be, how could it be!—

"Thinking of you two ladies here together will be a great satisfaction to me, Mrs. Hamilton," the Senator had told Aunt Carrie, that last day. "I am sure I could not leave this dear girl in better hands." He was smiling, patting her shoulder, hoping she wasn't going to cry. And Aunt Carrie was sweet; she just couldn't help being practical. "Not any more than I can, I suppose," Sabrina reflected. "Only I simply can't think about all those things Laura put up this summer without just wanting to die. And what good does that do anybody? Laura wouldn't like it, either. She would much rather people would eat them and say how good they were, and did she use her mother's recipe—and things like that."

Aunt Carrie was as natural about everything as if Laura had just gone off on a visit or gone to Washington with the Senator. "Did you say she hadn't been fretting about Rickie any more than usual lately—just before this happened, I mean? I used to think at first that maybe she oughtn't to be by herself, but she had overcome a lot of that. For Richard's sake more than her own, I dare say. So unselfish! And it was wonderful for her to have her winters away from here. I love the country as much as anybody; the whole year round too; but I have to admit the winter doesn't help you if you are feeling sad. Tell me about Washington, Sabrina. I was never there but once; twenty—no, more than that; nearer twenty-five—do you realize that's a whole quarter of a century ago? That's history, honey, that much time. Just count the Presidents! I thought it was an awfully pretty place and very interesting. I remember the Smithsonian Institution.

And naturally it has improved tremendously since then."

They talked about Washington: they went to a reception at the White House and witnessed an inaugural parade and took in the view from the Monument. And all the time Sabrina was thinking of Laura "by herself."

It was inevitable that the idea should be in everybody's mind; spoken or unspoken it was the first thing that had to be dealt with. She had been the one to do all the first things, and some of them had been hard; the questions most of all. When the Senator came he hardly asked her any, but she knew what he was thinking and she had tried harder than anything else to convince him that it was an accident. All the circumstances pointed to that. The doctor thought it was that, and so did she—and certainly he seemed to. And yet she was beginning now to see that there was no way ever to be free from this whispered suggestion. Knowing Laura, loving, adoring her, had nothing to do with it; not with the suggestion, though it might with the form it took. Aunt Carrie, for instance, had been natural about that just as she was about everything else—

"If I can only be natural too," Sabrina thought, "and not go imagining things that didn't happen, or that I have no way of knowing about. I seem to myself sometimes to be so dreadfully young. Inexperienced I mean of course; I could be just the same after I get to be fifty if I never had any experience. I know less about life, except housekeeping and things like that, than anybody living. I believe I know less about love than Laura did—and that is saying a good deal. Nora was educating her, though. That was one of the things they talked about. Nora was an expert on that subject."

How had it been possible, Sabrina wondered, for Laura not to guess in all that time that Nora must be terribly in love with somebody? Could she believe all that poetry and beauty and—and exaltation, were just for the Honorable Cecil? He was nice, of course, and supposed to be brilliant, but—Nora would have thought it funnier than anybody. It had seemed to Sabrina, right there at the last, just before the Digbys left, that she wasn't even trying to hide her feelings from him. It was a tremendous relief when they got away.

Inviolate. That was a word she would never hear

without thinking of Laura. Inviolate trust, inviolate innocence. Would it have been a terrible shock to her to find out what was going on in Nora's mind? Or would it not have shocked her in the least? Sabrina, who felt so far from being inviolate herself, could not take even this first step in her effort to analyze the situation. But it was an unusual situation; anybody would have to admit that. Her inexperience could not fool her into thinking this sort of thing went on very much. And certainly Laura had not seemed to be shocked up to the time the Digbys left, and since they came down here, there had only been Nora's letters. How many had she written to the Senator, Sabrina wondered, and what had he done with them—even with that one? There it was—the suggestion. For her, in spite of all she could do, it was taking that form; in spite of all the names she could give it—absurd, incredible, melodramatic. Nora was all of those things too. Who knew the kind of things she might put in a letter?

"If I can just get through Christmas!" She had said that many times. Not before Aunt Carrie, though; she wouldn't for the world let her know how she felt about it; any more than she would let Coq d'Or know.

They both kept chirping away from morning till night and she could at least pretend to be chirping too. All the same, winter in the country with an aching heart was bad enough without Christmas, which may have been intended for sad people as well as "merry" ones, but certainly made them sadder. Fire and sleet and candlelight—the Senator had reminded her of that in his last letter. "The coldest little poem in the world," he called it. "That fire doesn't warm it a bit, and the candlelight makes it worse. It is as flawless as an icicle. I have had it in my mind a good deal, these days that are so hard for both of us. It makes me hope, among other things, that Jake is bringing in plenty of wood and building beautiful fires for you and Mrs. Hamilton. I am sending all the holiday numbers of the various magazines. Lots of pictures for you to look at—"

Books, magazines, all the news he thought would interest her. He knew what it was like here without Laura. What it was like everywhere—

Henry was back for the holidays, with more ideas than ever. Bernard Shaw's this time. The trouble about associating with grown people was that it made the Henrys seem so young. "If I had a son right this minute, I would expect him to be as old as Henry," Sabrina thought. "I feel all the time that I am talking down to him. Not that he doesn't know a lot more than I do. Goodness yes! I couldn't begin to pass one of his examinations; but he never sees behind things; that through-the-looking-glass point of view the Senator has—that he has taught me to listen for. And his letters are exactly as if he were talking to me instead of writing."

With one big drawback, however: she couldn't ask him things. Questions sounded different in a letter, and answers *were* different. "All your friends remember you and ask to be remembered." He lumped them all together like that. "The Digbys are back, and, with all their transatlantic vibrations, they are naturally more in demand than ever." If she could talk to him Sabrina knew she would not let him stop there—with all the things she wanted to know about Nora! She had no idea how Nora would be affected by what had happened; nor how she would behave, under these changed conditions. She had already carried her several times from an abyss of genuine sorrow up through all the varying degrees of hypocrisy. How would a woman naturally feel if a thing like this happened to her? She would know how she ought to feel; any woman would know that; but would it be hard for her to do it? Not just a woman like Nora, but even an ordinary one in everyday life? Nobody would ever know, she supposed. They were the ones who kept their secrets. Nora was like the women in books, where the author can tell you everything about them. In most cases, however, the author was a man, so you might just as well imagine it for yourself. That is, if you could; if you had had enough experience—

She was glad Mr. Silvain was still in Washington. The Senator wrote more about him than anybody else. "I am learning a lot about art these days; these nights, rather. It's a good subject for discussion, provided there is only one artist in the party. If there are more, even one more, they either run into technicalities or a fight, and after that the poor layman can only look on. Silvain seems to think he may be able to do something about designing a monument for Rickie's grave, and Laura's, when his other work is finished. You remember she used to speak about wanting a statue of some kind: marble I suppose; we never went into the details very much. It seemed to me a matter that required more thought than we were able to give it—then. Now

I find myself thinking about it a great deal, and with Silvain to guide me—" Sabrina remembered how quiet the house on H Street used to be at night. They would be in the library, no doubt, with a fire in the grate and the green-shaded lamp on the desk. Mr. Silvain would probably be sitting there, drawing something. She could imagine the low voices, the long silences. It must be very interesting to both of them; it must be a sort of happiness. She believed that nothing could keep it from being that.

February in Washington was apt to be either the best or the worst month of the winter. This year it was still cold, but bright. The late sunshine fell under the trees into Lafayette Square and lay in long shafts of light beside their shadows on the snow, which was not enough to cover the grass but had refused to melt and still blew in little flurries along the walks, maintaining its whiteness by darkening everything else. Steele had noticed, as he turned to cross the Square, that the White House standing on its powdered lawn was no longer white.

When he went into the library he knew he would find Nora there. Jessie had met him in the hall and told him she had asked Mrs. Digby to go in there, where there was a good fire. "I told her you were liable to be home any minute now," Jessie said.

She was standing by the window. She had on a moleskin jacket and a little moleskin hat, and he thought when she turned toward him that he had never seen her look so well. Her cheeks were flushed, with walking, with the frosty air—or was it just the sunshine coming in? Now with the dark books behind her she seemed pale.

"Shall we sit over by the fire?" he asked her. "Are you cold?"

She shook her head. "I like you at your desk; then I can imagine I am not even here; that I am seeing you from somewhere else."

"With your second sight?" he asked. He was not smiling.

"Just that," she said. "You see how it came true."

They sat in silence for a while; he was looking down at the paper cutter in his hand, and Nora let her eyes wander about the room. "I was thinking," she said, bringing them back to his face, "what a curious thing it is for me to be sitting here in this room I have hardly ever been in before, and how hard it has been for me to come inside this house at all—who used to be here so much! Perhaps you have never thought how well you are protected from me. If I were a man and you a woman, I might at least ring your doorbell whenever I chose, but now I must not do so much as that; though I have done it, before today. Always you were not back yet from your office, since it had to be in the daylight that I came. Jessie will have told you; she was polite, but not approving. Even to you this must seem a curious thing."

He laid the paper cutter down and looked at her thoughtfully. "Men and women are curious things, Nora," he said. "They have a tremendous power of hurting one another. You spoke of that once yourself; do you remember? In so many ways. Nature—or shall we say God?—has put something between them that they are not permitted to forget. It takes a thousand forms, of beauty, and of danger—" She was looking at him with deep attention. He took up the paper-knife again. "You must remember they have had to make all sorts of rules to protect each other; like the rules in a game; it doesn't matter how clumsy they are if all the players agree on them—agree not to take advantage of their clumsiness—" The silence fell again.

"You did not answer my letter," she said after a while.

"No."

"Perhaps you did not even read it. Did you?"

"Yes. It made a little heap of ashes, Nora. You ought not to have written it; you know that."

"I had to write it; I wanted you to know those things. About the ashes it does not matter, if you read it; for now you know."

"Now I know," he said.

She did not speak at once, but sat thinking. She had taken off her little fur-lined gloves and was holding them in her lap. Her hands were very still.

"You talk about your rules—your game," she said after a while. "You admit it is a stupid game, or has grown to be one, though it may have started from all sorts of good intentions. It is like the things people do in church—the kneeling and the crossing—with their thoughts far away. They have forgotten why they do it, until some great trouble comes to teach them what is behind it all. Then in a flash it comes to them that God does not care at all for any of those rules. But you care; you go on caring. I believe I will never be able to understand how it is that you should care so much." She spoke with great intensity but without raising her voice from its habitual low key. This time there were no tears in it, nor in her eyes.

"It was the same," she went on, "when Laura was here and did not stand like a ghost between us. Many times she used to stand with me. She understood me many times when you did not, or pretended you did not. She knew more about me than you would believe, perhaps. Not that I loved you, though; that she could not have understood even if I had told it to her all day long. Her eyes were never made to see a thing like that; I think they would surely have gone blind before anything so splendid."

He was conscious again of that feeling of unreality she had evoked for him before. Did women say these things? Did they just sail directly into every convention, every precept of speech or conduct, without a glance at the compass or even at the stars? He had given much thought to love in the course of his life. He would have said he had learned enough about it, both through what he had accepted and what he had forgone, to insure his own tranquillity; to maintain his power of choice: that critical faculty in which he took such pride; the æsthetic awareness he had learned to trust. He had never expected to be looking into a mirage where past and future, here and there, life and death, were all one thing, to see the face of love. And where were right and wrong in this perspective—or even mine and thine?

They sat for some time without speaking. The sun was gone from the window now and the firelight had come into its own. It played with its reflection in the glass doors of the bookcases, with the bright objects on the desk, the rings on Nora's hands. The clock that stood on the mantel was in shadow, but presently it struck the hour. "You see," she said, when it had finished, "everything is against us. Not only that silly clock; not only Jessie and the cook downstairs, who will be getting your dinner ready, but the whole world outside. I believe there is no one out there on the street, even the most perfect stranger, who would not take this thing away from us: this peace, this nirvana. They do not want it to happen anywhere on earth, or even in heaven, because it makes them afraid. They are afraid of love that does not want to move anywhere again when it has found the thing it was seeking. In their hearts they know that then it would no longer make the world go round; it would make it stop; they could no longer have their time, their clocks. Do you remember in the Bible where it says there shall be no more time? When the angel said that, it was love he had in mind, to make such stillness."

She had risen and was buttoning up her jacket, drawing on her gloves, while he stood watching her. "But now I cannot be still, you see," she said, looking up at him with her unexpected smile.

Walking back in the cold twilight after seeing her to her door, it occurred to Steele, not for the first time, to question the superiority of things like reason, logic, and common sense in general, over some other qualities that might be considered their exact opposite. When it came to winning a moral or even a verbal victory, it was always possible to make some sort of stand against sound opinions, the kind that could be weighed and measured, even if one came out badly in the end; but the waking mind was defenseless in the beginning against the sort of reasoning carried on in sleep. The only way to refute a dream was to forget it. Its victory consisted in being a dream that one could not forget.

If only she could manage to get through the spring!
Down there where it all happened at once, rising the
way the Mississippi did, sweeping over you with no
levee to hold it back, it was always as much as the
heart could bear, and this year, it seemed to Sabrina,
it might easily be more. Spring was not good for sad
people either; but then, what was? "Tomorrow,"
some poet said, probably because it rhymed with
"sorrow." A great many things must have been written for reasons like that: because they rhymed, or were
alliterative, or sounded well in some other way. And
a lot of them had maybe turned out better than if they
had been written for some better reason. Tomorrow.
Just what was there to look forward to? She turned
off the soundless country road into a bridle path where
last year's leaves still rustled under her horse's feet.
She would come out presently into the cotton fields,
where she would have to pick her way home across
the dubious furrows. Surely no fields on earth held so
little promise as these down here. Who could ever believe the legends about the South, the ease, the afflu-
ence, if he were told it had been gathered from such
a prospect as the one that lay before her? She remem-

bered a story in the family about one of her mother's cousins who had gone to Paris and come home engaged to a French count. Everybody said it was for love on her side and money on his. Southern heiress. But when he came over to see for himself where the money came from, right in the middle of winter when stalks and mud were all anybody could see, he fled precipitately—so the story went. It took a lot of faith, agriculture did. Anything that depended on the Lord that much was bound to be uncertain—or at any rate prospective. Tomorrow was the word for that too.

Henry would be back for the spring vacation. She would at least have somebody to ride with her. If only it didn't mean so much more than that to him! It didn't seem fair for it to be just riding with her, when he kept writing as if it were the thing he was mainly living for. Romance. He was at just the right age for it; and she apparently never had been. She had never had a twinge of it, that she could remember. "Are you sure there isn't somebody up there in Washington?" he kept asking her; he evidently considered it had to be something like that to keep her from caring for him any more than she did. "Reciprocating" was Henry's word. Reciprocity. That did sound like Washington; like Congress. According to the paper, that was one of the things they were talking about just now: one of the "issues." Sabrina kept up with what was going on in Congress much more down here than she did in Washington. She remembered the way her father used to do. It was probably the people at home who were always more interested in politics. The Senator hardly ever mentioned anything that happened. Down here the papers gave his speeches in full. She wondered if Nora went to hear them. She always imagined her there, in the front row of the gallery, and when the paper said "applause," or "laughter," she could see Nora—

Mr. Silvain was going to do the statue himself, the Senator said. It would not be a statue exactly, but a figure in high relief, and in bronze instead of marble. The way he described it, it ought to be very unusual. Mr. Silvain was violently opposed to most of the things that were being done these days in sculpture; she had heard him talk about it. He was sarcastic and really rude, it seemed to her, and of course his own work was considered by a great many artists to be too unconventional and too advanced, and too ever so many other things. Sabrina intended to read up on it—the whole subject. She only knew the smooth classical things she had seen in museums and didn't even know how much she liked them. She was glad it was to be bronze though, instead of marble. More enduring than bronze. Horace was right about it. His verses had turned out to be entirely indestructible, so far as it was possible to judge; and that was a wonderful thing when you stopped to think of it. Beauty was responsible for that; not goodness, and not truth—whatever people meant by that. The Senator said you ought not to leave truth by itself that way; it always had to be *about* something. He said it was like the cipher in arithmetic: its value depended on what you put with it. Love, she supposed, was different. It was able to stand alone; it had at least the possibility of immortality, just as beauty had; it could be more enduring than bronze, too; depending, naturally, on how much eternity there was for anything.

"I do hope," Sabrina said, whispering the words almost as if it were a prayer she was saying to herself, out there in the wide loneliness of the cotton fields, "that nothing is ever going to happen to make me forget what I have learned about love, living with Laura and the Senator. No matter what people say, I have seen for myself that it can be perfect. And if anything goes on forever I know that will. I am glad they decided to have bronze instead of marble."

"It seems to me," Silvain said, "that it is about time to give up the idea that Americans worship money. There are few things any further from the truth. They haven't even a decent respect for money; look at the way they throw it around. Europe is where the jingle of the guinea calls the faithful to their knees; especially France. Americans, so far as I can see, don't worship anything. Even a golden calf might be better than that —than just letting the faculty become atrophied; after all, it's an ideal of a sort. Over here people seem to shrink from even the idea of an ideal. They won't look in any direction where they think they might see one —one of their own, that is."

Steele looked up from the drawings scattered over his desk with a smile. When Silvain got off like this it usually meant he would not get back on again for the rest of the evening: back on the subject that brought them together these days and made for him the principal interest in life. He began to put the sketches carefully together, as if they were already precious, the visible sign of a grace that haunted his imagination continually.

"When they begin creating things—I mean building them—with their money," Silvain went on, "they expect to get it done not only as well but as expensively as possible; to import the best artists; and even when they have an artist of their own they still import the ideals."

"Well, and if they didn't, what do you suppose it would look like?" Steele said.

Silvain shrugged. "God knows. But think of the fun they could have—here in a country where there are no ghosts to be outraged, no matter what they do."

"The ghosts have to be imported too, I suppose," Steele said. "Yet we manage to outrage something, every once in a while. Our trouble is probably the habit we have of mixing too many other considerations in with our art—practical considerations, like chastity and temperance. You remember what happened to MacMonnies's statue, his *Bacchante,* that had to be expelled from the Public Library in Boston?"

Silvain shrugged again. "Well, of course, when we get into the domain of sex I'll have to grant you a distinct originality. In that respect the American point of view is *sui generis;* we won't call it narrow; say specialized."

Steele reached for the cut-glass paperweight and set it on the little pile of drawings. The windows were open and the uncertain breath of spring moved through the room. "A friend of mine—he was from Boston too—used to lay it to our education; the elementary schools were too shy even to approach the question, he maintained, much less handle it. He said all his undergraduate work was done on the assumption that Venus was synonymous with vice and the Virgin with idolatry. At the time I knew him he was rather obsessed with a theory of woman as Force, a sort of rival of the dynamo."

"I wouldn't put it a bit beyond her," Silvain said. "All things to all men. It would certainly enhance her prospects over here to figure as energy instead of art. Draped in rays and vibrations, she would be allowed to stay in the Boston Library, I imagine." He picked up his sketches. "So you like what we've done so far. I'll remember your suggestion about the contrast being too sudden where the shadow of the drapery leaves off, there on the side of the face. But we must not forget what the outdoor setting is going to do in the way of light and shade. Trees and things. We can't allow for it, of course, but all the same we mustn't forget about it. As I remember, there was quite a large tree, a maple I think."

"Yes, a maple," Steele said.

"And then, of course, the seasons," Silvain went on. "Sometimes it's hard to know whether nature is for us or against us with these things. Her art is strictly kinetic, and when we try to introduce a static note she usually protests in one way or another. Certainly, you can't count on having it ever look the same, however dominant that idea may have been in the conception. The Unchanging. Not a bad name, if we wanted a name; which we don't, I believe."

Steele shook his head.

"Not even a family name, I think you said."

"None."

"Well, if it only comes up to the visions we have been indulging—yours and mine together—I'll feel more like an orchestra leader than somebody blowing a single horn. And even then I've got to see it out of the hands of my assistants. They simply can't keep from smoothing things. Sometimes I think every one of them, down to the carpenter that builds the scaffolding, must be an academician in disguise."

"—even the yellow ones, the whole ballet, before I had so much as heard the fiddles tuning up or seen the curtain moving; I had been thinking maybe it wouldn't move. And now when I cut across the parks they look at me reproachfully: *We have piped unto you and ye have not danced—*"

He had better not say too much about it, though; he didn't want to keep Sabrina from dancing; and besides, the spring down there was an old story by this time. He laid his pen across the glass inkwell and picked up the blotter.—Suppose the curtain hadn't moved: what good did a curtain do, any curtain, his lowered eyelids, his averted mind, when he knew all the time the dance was going on? What effigy of stillness was there to which even his smallest thought could cling, to be itself still—the Sphinx, the Pyramids? He could pile them all on top of it and it wouldn't help. He had been thinking about the Pyramids, since Silvain had spoken of the changing aspects of outdoor statuary, in the variations of light and shade to which it was subjected. Even without ever having seen the Pyramids he could imagine that to anyone who saw them a great deal—all the way from sunrise to moonset—they would probably register more changes even than the sea. Apparently there was no symbol of any kind that could help to steady the moving show. No emblem.

It might surprise a good many people, Steele thought, if they were told that their sorrows were as inveterately transient as their joys. For some reason the human race had long ago abandoned joy to be regarded as the counterpart of all that was most fleeting and put its hopes of permanence in pain. Surely despair must be dependable! Poor despair, already on the bottom with nowhere to go but up.

"The more I think of it, Sabrina, the more convinced I am that not dancing is always a mistake. I believe if we listened as attentively as we should to all the whispers going on, outside of us and in, and all the answers, we would know that we are not going to be allowed any rest anyway, and so, since move we must, we might as well do it to music. In a young and pliant fashion, naturally, as long as we can, and after that just the best we can, but still rhythmically, even if our back hurts—or creaks a little, like an ancient tree. Iambic pentameter, you notice; inadvertent, but it might prove something, if we only knew what."

No rest for the sole of one's foot. Motion could be thought of as ineluctable, he supposed, or even blind, but when it came to beating out a measure or following a figure— The foot had to have something besides a sole before it could make a pattern for itself; there had to be a head attached—somebody's head. Choice entered there—somebody's choice. He never had seen the point in sticking for free will until we knew a little more about what we were doing, or wanted to do; or, for that matter, what we had already done. History. He had a friend who taught history, at Harvard. History was incoherent and immoral—he had heard him say it a dozen times—and had either to be taught that way or falsified. Steele did not believe it could ever be written in that spirit; nobody would want to do it. The only reason for writing history, it seemed to him, was this very idea of tracing out a pattern, sequence at least if not harmony, in the welter of events. The same motive was probably back of any kind of writing—biography, fiction, drama—the form could be anything, or the material; men found their experiences and their ideas about equally chaotic, he supposed, and the importance of getting them into some kind of shape equally great. In one way or another they were obliged to do something with the mystery of their lives; they had to think their way through somehow, or just give up thinking altogether. Or give up living—

It was an accident, of course: what the doctor called an accident. In some unreal interval that was neither sleep nor waking she must have repeated the dose; the uncovered box, the glass of water, were there on her little table; she had only to put out her hand. If they had known sooner; if he had not been away— What was the pattern here? For those four years he had watched her steadily, quietly turn her face toward the west—the wide exit: *The dark will end the dark, if anything.* He could not point her to the east; was there some way to lead her? What had he left undone?

"At all events, from now on you are at liberty to picture me as moving metrically about my business, not only through the parks but even in waste places like the Senate. You tell me you are more interested in what goes on there than you used to be. Someone remarked recently, in a burst of national pride, that this country was strong enough to carry even its politics, so you may be strong enough to read about them, but don't do it too much; I would rather think of you on horseback.

"I am glad Henry recalls our last year's arguments in a way that makes him want to come at me again, but you report his arsenal bristling with such modern and explosive weapons that it makes me tremble for the old flintlock."

The house on H Street had taken on the leafy, shaded look it wore in summer: an effect largely borrowed from the trees across the way, but contributed to by an elm tree of its own, whose branches brushed the upstairs windows on that side. The library was on that side, and now with its windows open it might have been almost anywhere in the country, Steele thought gratefully when he came into it in the late afternoons.

All his life, it seemed to him, he had had to struggle for whatever intervals of solitude he had managed to put into it. He could not remember a time when he had not had to practice all sorts of evasions—not all of them creditable, he was afraid—in order to be alone. He had been led to attach a value to the simple absence of his fellow man that had no relation whatever to the use he proposed to make of it. Coming into his library these first warm days, he realized with a pang that here at last with no need for further scheming was the green thought in the green shade. How did men spend the treasure for which their breasts were wrung?

For several weeks following Nora's visit he had felt it as a disturbing influence. Almost he had expected to see her when he opened the door, by the window where she had been standing, in the chair he had placed for her, with the rows of his dark books behind her vivid face. The dream had faded now; the door stood open all the time; he could see there was nobody there. He had seen her now and then in other places, but not again alone.

It interested him to discover that as further invasion on her part in either a real or an imagined form began to seem less and less likely to him, he was apt to recall the more evanescent aspects of their interview as if they were important to its meaning: impressions of voice and movement that for some reason he did not want to forget. It was an experience in depth only, adding no new element of understanding to the situation. How deep could one go in plumbing a nature like that? What echoes would he waken, in what caves? It seemed to him now that he had noticed almost in the beginning of his acquaintance with her how little surface it presented. In most social relations one seemed able to proceed almost indefinitely in two dimensions; with Nora there was always the sudden drop, the water closing over one's head, as if one were expected to sail or swim not on the top but on the bottom of a lake.

"Mrs. Digby was here, sir, a little while before you came in." Jessie, who had come upstairs to give him this information, stood in the doorway looking, it seemed to him, a little apologetic for some reason.

"I am sorry, Jessie," he said. "Did she leave a message for me?"

"Only that she couldn't wait. I took her into the parlor, but she said she wanted a book out of the library, so she came up here. Then I heard her coming down again, and that time she said she couldn't wait. I asked her about the book—if I could help her find it —but she didn't say anything."

"Thank you, Jessie," he said, turning back to the letter he was writing. What were the soundings here? He would have liked to ask a few more questions, but better not; there were deep places in Jessie too.

The letter was one to Sabrina he had started the day before. He glanced at the clock; he would finish it and get it in the box in time for the six o'clock collection.

As he walked back from the corner he saw a boy jump off his bicycle and start up the steps. The note he handed him was from Nora: She must see him; could he come that evening—at any hour?

Between six o'clock and eight, particularly if a man is dining alone, he has time to cover a pretty broad field of speculation on almost any subject. The field in this case seemed to Steele practically unlimited because he had been given nothing whatever by which to define it. He could not even be sure of the plane on which his imagination was expected to function; it had been called upon before to transcend the boundaries of time and space. Inevitably his mind returned to that other occasion when Nora had seen, or imagined that she saw, here in his house, something that frightened her. Until he should have an explanation of her conduct this afternoon, it was bound to seem to him some sort of repetition of the former experience. What was this curious bond between them that apparently made it possible for her to be aware of things concerning him to which he was entirely blind? Not the events themselves; he was not willing to concede that the awareness extended to regions outside the subjective, but what other regions were there that concerned him so profoundly as the shadowy places in his own soul?

He found her already waiting for him; there was no indication that she intended to do anything but wait: no book, no work, no evening paper; nothing less futile than time itself to keep her company. She looked very slight, very pale, in the blue shadows of the room as she came forward to meet him. "Sit here," she said, taking the other corner of the blue sofa. "Now we can look at one another." And, this preliminary accomplished, "I have two things to tell you."

"Yes?" he said.

"Both of them I learned today: one is that we are to be sent to China; to Pekin; soon, Cecil thinks; and the other is that I shall not kill myself as I planned to do if a thing like this should happen. You knew that;

I had told you that I did not want to live when I could not even see you any more. It was to tell you again that I went to your house this afternoon; did Jessie tell you I was there?"

"Yes," he said. He knew it was all she expected him to say. He did not have to speak at all; he was going down, down—

"I went upstairs into the library—to get something to read, I told Jessie—but I did not know why I went. Now I do know, and it was something to read after all: I read the letter lying open on your desk. That is how I know it would be useless to kill myself; I know now there is no way I can be near you even if I die."

"But, Nora—"

"It may surprise you that I should do a thing like that; I wonder sometimes what I would not do. And yet, even so, it was only the page you left lying up that I read, and not the others. Perhaps I did not need the others to teach me what it was intended that I should know."

"But, my dear Nora—" His amazement would not let him be silent, yet what was there he could say, so far beyond his depth? What was there on that page "lying up"—so open in every sense of the word—

that could lead to this profound misunderstanding?

She shook her head. "No, I am not mistaken. It was not a love-letter; I know that; surely I am not a fool. It is because my wisdom in these things is greater than yours that you must listen to me. When a man casts out a temptation, as they say, do you believe it is to leave an empty place behind it in his soul? The soul would not permit a thing like that; he would never do it except for something he wants more—because it is more daring, perhaps, or only because it is more safe; but no matter what it is, it is for him his soul's desire; it holds the place of love."

Again there was no answer that seemed possible to him. If he told her she was mistaken, it would tell her more than that; he could deny nothing without affirming things he had no right to let her believe.

She might have been waiting for this denial; there was silence between them. "You see," she said at last, "for you I am not safe, and so I have been cast out. Another woman in such a case might be very desperate. I believe she would even feel that she must kill somebody; but I shall not even kill myself, because I know it would be useless; the soul must choose its path."

He was aware that his position had become intolerable. He was not a deity, a cross-legged idol, to sit here in silence, breathing incense. No code of behavior could impose a situation like this on any man alive. Even allowing for the fact that neither the behavior nor the code had been developed on the assumption that such a situation could arise, there should nevertheless be some way to cope with it, since it had arisen. So long as he had been able to picture himself as the victim of a mysterious attraction—as a decently drowning man—he had managed to view his predicament with some slight measure of sympathy; but now—

All at once, with the retrospective clarity the idea of drowning had suggested, he was able to see why at any rate the abnormal circumstance in question should be his and not another's, even if he still saw no way to handle it. He had brought it on himself; it was the nemesis of that reality he had rejected all his life. He could not remember a time when he had not gloried in escaping from it by every means in his power. As a boy, as a student presumably occupied with such serious considerations as philosophy, it had been an amusement and a delight to him to leap the dilemmas and even the temptations in his path by swinging up on something, some overhanging branch the forest of his imagination provided—a monkey-like practice that he had found exceedingly convenient and liked to think of as being in a way ancestral. Well, he must have swung up too often. What he found now in the path before him had brought the forest with it; he was going to be forced to deal on terms of some sort of reality with the logic and the language of a dream. The temptation here was to let go. Surely so unswerving a partisan of the ideal could claim the right to hold at last a vision to his breast? He knew better. He had been too long the champion of such promises not to have learned that unfulfillment was the sign by which their votaries knew them.

"I wonder if you know," he said at length— "if you have any idea how difficult you make it for me not to tell you that you are mistaken about many of the things you have said, however right you may be about the others. But let us just assume that you are right about them all: about the things that I have chosen and the ones I have chosen to do without. We will even assume that the ways we both have taken must from now on take us far apart. I believe that will make it easier for me to say whatever I can say without the risk of—of getting us into an argument, or of hurting you in some other way. It is not much, I am afraid, but to say anything at such a time ought to be considered a great privilege; just think what a man who had missed such a chance would give to have it over! He might be willing to come back and go through the trouble of dying all over again, to be able to tell someone how lovely she had been, and how kind— and to tell her not to cry, Nora, because he wasn't worth it—indeed, indeed he never could have been."

The things Henry said about Freud impressed Sabrina as being altogether unsuitable for general conversation, however interesting they might be in a classroom. At Easter they had had Bernard Shaw, who was advanced enough, in all conscience, but funny. Henry had read *Man and Superman* out loud to her and they had both enjoyed it tremendously, but now if she even smiled at Freud he was offended. She didn't like to tell him it wasn't because Freud struck her as being the least bit amusing, but simply because she was embarrassed. The psychology of the unconscious seemed to explain practically everything for Henry, and to excuse most of it. Apparently you could own to any suggestion, however disgraceful, if it was wandering about in your "unconscious." How did you know where it was, or how long you could keep it there? Anyhow, it gave him something to talk about besides wanting to marry her. She was already two years older than Henry, and by the time he finished at the university it would be at least twenty.

"What's two years?" Aunt Carrie said. "Good-looking, good family, college-bred—what more do you want? And money enough too, I suppose. I believe Washington must have spoiled you." She could tell by the way Aunt Carrie looked at her that she was another one who thought there must be somebody in Washington—

Nobody in Washington; nobody here; and now she was going to New Orleans for the winter, and maybe to Europe next summer. "How wonderful!" That was all she heard on every side, and yet she couldn't think about it without a terrible ache somewhere—in the unconscious maybe, because certainly with her mind she knew it really was wonderful. It was her favorite aunt, her father's sister, this time who had invited her. "Nobody else can possibly need you as much as I do,

Sabrina. The girls are just at the right age to grow up like you, which is exactly what I want them to do." It was really as a sort of companion to the girls that Aunt Eunice wanted her, though of course she would never call it that. Sabrina couldn't call it that either, not even to herself, without taking a good long look ahead of her. She didn't want to be one of those people that other people couldn't do without; she had known too many of them; the South was rather full of them. Still, it was about the only way she would ever get to Europe, or to New Orleans either, for that matter.

Would she ever stop feeling that this was home— the one place in the world that she couldn't bear to leave? And yet she hadn't minded when they went to Washington—because they went together, of course. It was really Laura and the Senator that were home.

It was late summer now. Cotton-picking. Poor Mr. Murray had been simply desperate over the way things were going. The Negroes were twice as much trouble when they began to get their money and to drink it up and waste it in all sorts of ways. They wouldn't have a red cent of it left by Christmas, Mr. Murray said. There had been all sorts of filibusters and postponements in Congress, and now that the Senator had finally got here, he was away almost all the time.

The statue had come before he did, and had to wait to be put in place. He had all the directions from Mr. Silvain—sketches and things. It was finished now and the maple tree behind it was beginning to turn. Lovely, lovely! Sabrina didn't believe there could be anything in Europe, ancient or modern, as beautiful as that. It made people want to cry; not only the ones who knew about it, but complete strangers. She had seen them stand there and dab their eyes with their handkerchiefs; women, of course, but the men looked serious too. They all had different ideas about what it meant. Laura's friends tried to imagine the figure was intended to look like her— "Not a portrait statue, of course, but there is something of her there—" How could there fail to be something of Laura in anything so beautiful in that quiet sort of way?

"Wouldn't you say *Resignation,* Sabrina, more than anything else?" Aunt Carrie said. "What did Mr. Silvain say it meant?"

"I don't believe he ever said, Aunt Carrie. I am sure the Senator never did. I believe they think a work of art can only mean what people want it to mean; a sort of answer to some question they ask for themselves; it is different for everybody."

"Well, it's beautiful, but I must say it looks like Laura to me," Aunt Carrie said.

Even the Senator didn't take Henry seriously, though he always pretended to feel sorry for the boys she didn't like.

"The trouble with these youngsters, Sabrina—"

"It's with me," she said. "They seem to feel exactly the way they are expected to, about their life, and about what they call their dreams. With me, for some reason, it's all life; the dreams got left out; I'm just not romantic."

He looked at her. "No, I suppose not—in terms of Henry. You see, romance is pretty comprehensive; it's a wide country; people live in different quarters of it; different views, different languages. We can't talk about it profitably until we find whether we are all talking about the same thing. We might have a debate about that some time, the three of us. Everybody is romantic according to some definition, it seems to me."

"I wonder what yours is," Sabrina said.

"I am going to tell you when I have time. Am I ever going to have time for anything, Sabrina? I would hate to let you go off to New Orleans, much less to Europe, without complete specifications on a matter as important as that. My point of view, naturally. You already have yours, and Henry can give us Freud's."

He wasn't going to have time. But he wouldn't do it anyhow. Maybe he didn't have to; maybe she knew already. Romance for the Senator didn't have any more to do with love than it did with a lot of other things. It was the way you looked at them—even loss, even sorrow. Where did people ever get the idea that being in love was bound to be romantic? Henry, for instance.

Nora, of course, was different. Sabrina admitted there was something romantic about Nora whether she was in love or not. She still thought a good deal about Nora; it seemed to her she ought somehow to know a little more about the end of that story—which might be said to have ended, she supposed, since the Digbys were going to China. In a way, she had a sort of right to know how Nora had been taking all of these tremendous changes; after all, she had been the one to call the Senator's attention to how Nora felt about him and to put him a little on his guard. But he hardly ever mentioned her and never under any circumstances took one of the openings she gave him: whether Nora was glad to be going back to the Orient, for instance; or whether they would be likely to hear from the Digbys any more.

Those openings had seemed to Steele amusing and rather touching. Sabrina was such an odd mixture of innocence and wisdom. Funny her father should have hit on that name for her— He had noticed before that children who had not been given the responsibility of a family name were apt to listen to the name itself— to take a hint from it, so to speak. Though the hint was given to them in their blood, no doubt; why shouldn't a parent's taste be inherited just as well as the color of his eyes? It was such a mysterious business anyway; why limit it in one direction rather than another?

To a man of her father's age—of his own age now— there was naturally a very great charm in such an antithesis, a charm that the men of her age would scarcely be aware of. Would they be aware of it in Europe—France, for instance? Even a younger man in an older country— Yet it seemed to him so typically American.

He was going to miss it. He was going to miss a lot of things. He wanted to tell her about them if he could do it without making these last weeks too elegiac—without making her protest too much: "Nothing can ever make me feel different. In spite of all you say, I know there are some things that simply cannot change!" How the old lie deceived us, as long as we were young. And when we stopped believing it, what had we gained except the knowledge that we were old? But old or not, he knew a parting when he saw one, and death had less to do with it than people imagined.

It had been a sweet companionship; he was glad to realize that he had known its value all along. It was always humiliating to see the brightness only at the end. Dear child, dear girl, that walkest with me here— No, not Wordsworth. She wasn't one of his girls. If her father had named her Lucy—

Safe.—Who was it said the most beautiful word in the language was "secure"? It would have to be the most beautiful one in all languages then, its meaning alone being considered, and meaning the same thing to everybody, however variously they might proceed about getting hold of something they could apply it to. Women were notoriously bad risks, but why shouldn't another human being of any description be the most forlorn hope of security imaginable? Nobody looked for it in himself; he knew it wasn't there. The man who looked for it in Sabrina would be able at least to gauge his chances with a fair degree of accuracy. Which was probably what Nora meant.

No, he didn't believe they would be likely to hear from the Digbys very often, he told Sabrina. "China is a long way round, you know. Enormously interesting too, especially for someone as sympathetic with the spirit of the Orient as Nora is—or as they both are, for anything we know to the contrary. Cecil keeps his sympathies so well bottled up; I suppose a diplomatist never has to get at one of them in a hurry. They liked him in Washington, though. You never heard of so many farewell parties—"

He had been glad to hear of them himself; to learn from the daily papers that the charming Mrs. Digby had been daily visible in some quarter, beautiful and admired. He did not like to think of her as he had been obliged to leave her, her face still hidden in the blue brocaded pillow.

Sabrina was sitting on the top step of the front porch looking down the driveway between the yellowing trees. She wondered how long it would be before somebody, white or black, on foot or on horseback or in a buggy, would turn in at the gate and come casually up to lay the afternoon in ruins. It was so peaceful without anybody; with Aunt Carrie taking her Sunday nap and the Senator reading his Sunday paper and her sitting here doing her Sunday nothing! And so few Sundays left. But she wasn't going to start counting them, like Laura.

"I wish—" she said, turning her head toward the window behind her as Steele stepped through it out on the porch, but she did not go on. He sat down by the column at the other end of the worn wooden step and looked at her inquiringly. "Transitive verb, I believe?"

"Nothing," she said. Somebody was turning in at the gate.

"Looks like Tom Dickenson, doesn't it? Your eyes

are better than mine," he said. "Well, I know what he wants. Don't go in."

Sabrina had seen business transacted on the bottom step before. A top-step audience never interfered in the least with either its pattern or its tempo. "Good evening, Tom." "Good evenin', Miss Sabrina." After which her presence would be ignored as in a Chinese play. This time the business was a new roof for Tom's dwelling and was quickly dispatched.

"Viney say she don't res' so good when it rains, the way she have to keep gettin' up an' jerkin' the bed aroun'," Tom had explained.

"With him in it, I suppose," Steele said as he departed. "Do you remember the story about the fisherman's wife who started wishing for improvements and ended by living in the Emperor's palace—or was it the Vatican?

Flounder, flounder in the sea—

I hope we are not starting Viney off on that sort of a career, with her new roof. You were about to do a little wishing yourself, weren't you?"

"Yes, but I saw it wouldn't do any good. I was wishing nobody would come. It's so nice when they don't."

222

They both looked off under the trees, then back at each other. "It is nice, isn't it?" he said.

"Did you ever think, Sabrina," he began presently, "what a lot of literature has grown up around that idea of making a wish, or having three wishes? It isn't the same as just wanting things; that may be reprehensible, as ambition or envy, but it doesn't have the sort of fatal catch in it that the wishing business has. They generally show the man, or the woman—for some reason they nearly always make it a woman—with the three wishes having to spend both the last ones getting rid of whatever she got with the first one. It's really a fascinating idea; it's a little like the fable about the lies people tell turning out to be true. Those things always appeal to me for some reason; I suppose because I have got into the habit of watching for them. You find them in all languages, I imagine; they must go pretty deep."

He looked so nice and peaceful, Sabrina thought, sitting there thinking about things that appealed to him—thinking out loud.

"Fear, of course, is at the bottom of most fables, legends, or whatever you call them; they are meant to carry a warning. Folklore seems to be pretty generally founded on fear. But then the question comes in: what is the fear founded on? There must be a rather firm conviction in people's minds that things, facts, are likely to turn out in some such way if we don't watch them—or if we do, for that matter. About all the good watching does is just to let us in a little on what is happening; I doubt if we can change it very much, no matter how much we know about it. Makes it more interesting as a spectacle, though."

"You talk as if everything turns out wrong—as if there were nothing we wouldn't like to change," Sabrina said.

"There is nothing that isn't going to change, whether we like it or not. What we don't like is to have it change without our consent—before we are ready for it. I wonder sometimes if we understand enough about what is going on even to be in the audience. With this idea in our minds of holding up the show whenever we get ready we must be a good deal of a nuisance. Our system is to sit down on the ruins of something and make comparisons, instead of letting the play go on—which it is going to do anyhow. Maybe we ought to leave memory to the poets, along with a lot of other things. Sorrowful Sequence —that's a nice name for a poem; and it's really just another name for the way we look at things. And proud of it too. Constancy. Where did we pick up that virtue in the first place, I wonder, with nothing to teach it to us—nothing outside ourselves. There's none of it in nature, certainly, and no regrets either— not one in the whole cosmos. In the autumn, for instance, when we go in so for the pathetic fallacy and talk so much about the end of things, what they are really doing is starting over. Anybody that lives in the country is bound to know that; certainly you can't run a farm on any other basis. *That maketh all things new*—That doesn't fit in very well with remembering all the old ones, does it? What if it turned out that God was more interested in forgetting than in forgiving? How do you feel about it?"

Sabrina's eyes in sunlight were amber like her hair and her freckles, but in shadow, especially the shadow of her own thoughts, they were darker, they were brown. Steele had noticed this change come over them as he was speaking. "I don't believe you agree with me," he said.

225

"I don't believe you want me to; I don't believe you agree with yourself when you talk that way. You sound—" She hesitated.

"All right," he said, "I am ready; let's have it."

"You sound as if you were trying to play safe—to propitiate something: destiny, God maybe. I don't know whether you are doing it for yourself or just for me—because you don't want me to expect too much from life, or love perhaps, and be disappointed."

He looked at her, surprised. The freckles had disappeared under the wave of color in her cheeks. He had no idea he had touched the springs of such earnestness. One never knew, till suddenly she flew that flag. He had sometimes amused himself by thinking what a temptation it might be to a man, a lover—provided he had any sense—to experiment with the causes of such visible commotion in this young creature's blood. There must be a key, a scale, for an instrument like that. If one had the right to learn it—

"I wish you wouldn't worry about me," she said. "I know what life is for most people, and love too. You think I don't—I know I don't sound as if I knew very much about things like that except from books, but I do. I've thought about them ever since I can re-

member, and I know that what you always say about
not being able to find perfection anywhere, or to keep
it, even if we did—I know that is true for practically
everybody. And yet all the time I have heard you saying this, you have been showing me something different—" Her voice, her color, died away. The dia-
pason came to a full stop.

Guessing what she had set herself to say to him,
and at the effort it would take, he would have liked to
forestall it. "I believe I know what you mean, because
I know you so well, Sabrina, but I am afraid that what
it really amounts to is that you have given too wide a
meaning to a rather special instance—to a very fortunate—"

"That is just it," she broke in—"because it is so rare,
and because I have been so fortunate as to know about
it—to live these years with you and Laura! I know it
is a funny thing to say, but I believe—"

"Yes?"

"I mean I am sure—"

"Think it out, Sabrina; you don't have to tell me
now."

"But I have thought it out; I have been wanting to
tell you all this time—I used to feel like telling Laura

—that I understood even better than she did how perfect it was. She didn't realize how different such a love was—is—from what people usually mean; she expected to be loved like this—as if it were God loving her. Even if you had tried to convince her she could ever lose it, by changing, by dying, even, you could not have done it. And the very idea of Nora or anybody—"

She was watching him to be certain he understood the spirit in which she offered him these things—this bread, this wine. Reassured, she went on: "You see, Laura did not have to think about it very much, but I did; because I was outside of it, and because of these things you are always saying about love and beauty and all the other ideals—that they were not even intended to last and we are foolish to expect them to. I wish you wouldn't try to fool me that way any more. I believe the thing that would make me the happiest— that would keep me from minding so much about going away—would be for you to treat me as if you knew I understood."

"My dear child—" he began.

"No, don't call me a dear child. Don't explain anything to me. All I want you to do is to feel that you can talk to me about what you really think—what you really believe—as you would to someone you could trust—someone like Mr. Silvain. He must have seen exactly what you meant. When I look at the statue it is just as if he had had nothing to do with it—only you. And how can you go on saying it is a mistake to remember and to cling to beautiful things, when you have put that there to show to prove—"

"To prove how impossible it is to do otherwise? If you were Silvain I might tell you that. That is something on which we can all agree," he said gently. "There are lots of things. I am going to agree with you right now that I have been thoughtless and rather foolish many times to say the things I have. It is a habit I fell into long ago—a habit of following my thoughts instead of directing them, just to see where they would lead me, and since I have had you to listen to me I have made it worse by doing it aloud. Which ought to show you that I do trust you," he said, smiling. "Nobody would let himself go like that before someone he didn't trust; we can agree on that point too, can't we?"

She knew it was over, and she didn't think she had won very much. Maybe not anything. She might even have made it impossible for him to talk to her at all,

which was something she could hardly bear to contemplate. But then she couldn't bear it the other way
either—to have him go on speaking so lightly of the
things she knew were most sacred to him. It shut her
out so, it was like a curtain let down between them.

Somebody else was coming in at the gate; a buggy
this time; but it did not matter so much; the afternoon
was ruined anyhow.

"It's Dave Mitchell," Steele said, getting up. "I told
him I would go with him to look at that drainage
ditch. I'm going to think about what you've told
me, Sabrina. Whether I ever find an answer to your
charges or not, I'm glad you made them. I don't want
that better nature of mine—or the one you think you
would like better—to fail you entirely if I can help it.
And whether you like it or not"—he turned to smile
at her from the bottom step—"you are a dear child."

Who is Sylvia? what is she?—

He had begun by whistling it, but now the words
were demanding attention. How many years had it
been since he had sung that song—or any song? It
would be an interesting study in association—if he

didn't always have to be thinking about something else as he rode about the country—to figure out just why certain airs, odd bits of music or of verse, came back to him at certain places. No doubt because he once put them into action at that particular spot, singing or declaiming them at that bend in the road, that view of the river. He used to be very vocal about his impressions in those days; probably made tracks in his brain for them to run on, according to—whose new theory of memory had he been reading?— And who was Sylvia?—

> *Is she kind as she is fair?*
> *For beauty lives with kindness—*

No doubt there was a track in his brain for that idea to run on, too, back in those days; it would never have occurred to him to question the truth of a little thing like that. Now he knew it was not only far from being true, but very far indeed from being a little thing.

He stopped his horse and looked about him. "I take this spot—that oak tree, that telegraph pole—to mark a new impression—" He wasn't saying it aloud though, so perhaps it wouldn't register. At any rate, he was all at once convinced that if beauty and kindness could be induced to live together inseparably, it would be about the only arrangement necessary to insure everybody's happiness. Such a simple and comprehensive arrangement too; it would take care of practically everything, even love, which, since it followed beauty like the tide, would now be constrained to follow kindness. Certainly a departure from the past. Eros the cruel-hearted; no more flaming torches for poor old Eros. What would he be in the revised version? *Agape*—Charity? Though I speak with the tongues of men and of angels—his definition varied in all of them. And not only a "thousand thousand voices," but a thousand faces too. When it came to kindness, though, people seemed to know what they were talking about.

And when it came to him, if he had any sense, he would let things like that alone. He would take the next bend in the road to register the indelible conviction that an ordinary man had no business experimenting with nebulous ideals. They ought to be left to the professional idealists, who were more or less under suspicion anyhow and didn't run the same risk of being followed and getting not only themselves but other people into trouble. The so-called practical man owed it to everybody to be practical; to stick to the street called Straight, and not go wandering off into the ones labeled Impasse.

All the same, Sabrina had done more than just follow him. She had outdistanced him entirely; gone where he never dreamed of leading anybody. And now he didn't know what he was going to do about it.

Too practical. Too unromantic—she believed that. He had meant to tell her before she went away that she was the most inordinately romantic human being alive. He had meant to tell her lots of things. Dear child, dear girl, that walkest with me here— He had known it was over, but not like this; he had not realized until that conversation on Sunday what an impossible situation she was leaving him in: so crowned with virtue, so encumbered with attributes, that he couldn't move in any direction without bringing something down with a crash. They were bad too, those crashes. Somebody always got hurt. Better keep still and let time handle it: time, the curse and the cure.

But how many years of her life might she waste in this absurd business, comparing her young lovers— comparing everybody—with that type of perfection in her mind that she had chosen him to represent? The word was always being made flesh, or stone—or bronze. Even God couldn't keep us from idolatry. Maybe He didn't want to. Why had He made the world if He didn't like images? They were exactly what He did like, only He wanted them to be used properly; He didn't like them frozen. *This shall be thus no more.* It was written over the door of the temple, over the altar. For love and laughter, for adoration and for tears, every moment was the last.

Such, at this bend of the road, were his findings. He here proclaimed himself the apostle of impermanence. But that wasn't going to keep Sabrina from taking him as the symbol of constancy. She was to all appearances going to steer by him as unswervingly as if he were the Great Bear in person. If he failed her, the constellation would undoubtedly collapse. Well, he must not fail her.

Sabrina fair, and kind—and safe. Nora had not been the only one to offer him an outline of his future. Apparently no psychic endowments were required for friends, servants, neighbors, to see what lay ahead of him, and—discreet and vague in varying degrees according to their various codes—to point it out to him. Circumstances, nature herself, might be said to indicate it. Sabrina alone had obviously missed the obvious. Somebody would have to shout it in her ear. For this, he hoped, it was still, by everybody's code, too soon; they would let her get away unenlightened. And then how soon, by everybody's code, would it already be too late? This too could be safely left to time—the curse, the cure, the convenience.

And since he knew so well what was in everybody's mind except his own, perhaps he did not have to investigate that shadowy precinct very closely on this occasion. It was apt to be too soon or too late for anything he was likely to discover there. Whether he might some day have wanted Sabrina to love him, whether she loved him now—for these and other questions the time had never come, and was already past. He was not going to enter any race with the sort of rival she had set up for him. He knew too well which was the better man.

"Aunt Carrie said she thought you might come to Italy next summer when we are there." Sabrina's voice was cheerful, as befitted the last Sunday. "I wonder what made her think so. It sounds like a wish coming true, but why would she be wishing it—"

"Instead of me?"

"Did you tell her—?"

He shook his head. "Only that I couldn't. Afraid even to wish it; you remember what I told you about wishes being dangerous. Besides, what would become of the Democratic Party—to say nothing of the plantation?" He looked at her reflectively. "I must have been just about your age when I was in Rome that summer. Nobody much older than that ought to be allowed in Rome."

"Why? Because they—"

"Because they don't take it in the right spirit any longer—as pure emotion. They think they have to think about it; history-conscious; like Gibbon. I had a friend who used to teach history. He said Rome was a flat contradiction of everything he had ever taught. There was nothing like a time sequence to be deduced from it; you could take its history either forward or backward; it had been everything and was going to be everything else—including America. Eternal City in that sense anyhow; for him."

"And was it for you—in any sense—when you were my age, I mean?"

"Yes, my sense; the eternity of a dream. Actual eternity, so long as we don't wake up."

"And have you now?—waked up, I mean. Is that why you don't want to go back? Because you are afraid—" She stopped, but the rising color kept on, the bright signal whose meaning had never been quite clear to him.

"Afraid of waking others," he said; "making too much noise; talking too much. I am going to cure myself of that while you are away. I won't have anybody to talk to then, you see, so it ought to be easy."

"All the same, I wish—" He waited while the signal was withdrawn.

"Don't," he said, smiling at her, shaking his head—"too dangerous."

THIS BOOK IS SET IN GRANJON

a type named in compliment to Robert Granjon, type-cutter and printer—Antwerp, Lyons, Rome, Paris—active from 1523 to 1590. The boldest and most original designer of his time, he was one of the first to practise the trade of type-founder apart from that of printer.

This type face was designed by George W. Jones, who based his drawings upon a type used by Claude Garamond (1510 61) in his beautiful French books, and more closely resembles Garamond's own than do any of the various modern types that bear his name.

This book was composed, printed, and bound by H. Wolff, New York.

The typography is by Stefan Salter